MATED to the PRINCE

Portal City Protectors Book 3

GEORGETTE ST. CLAIR
LETEISHA NEWTON

Mated to the Prince
(Portal City Protectors Book 3)
Text copyright © 2019 Georgette St. Clair & LeTeisha Newton

All Rights Reserved in accordance with the U.S. Copyright Act of 1976, the scanning, uploading, and electronic sharing of any part of this book without the permission of the publisher or author constitute unlawful piracy and theft of the author's intellectual property. If you would like to use material from this book (other than for review purposes), prior written permission must be obtained by contacting the publisher at info@beyonddeflit.com. Thank you for your support of authors' rights.

FBI Anti-Piracy Warning: The unauthorized reproduction or distribution of a copyrighted work is illegal. Criminal copyright infringement, including infringement without monetary gain, is investigated by the FBI and is punishable by up to five years in federal prison along with a fine of $250,000.

This book is a work of fiction. Any references to historical events, real people, or real places are used fictitiously. Other names, characters, places, and events are products of the author's imagination, and any resemblance to actual events or places or persons living or dead is entirely coincidental.

Beyond DEF
https://www.beyonddeflit.com

Editing – Tiffany Fox; Beyond DEF
Cover design – LeTeisha Newton; Beyond DEF
Interior Layout & eBook Adaptation: Deena Rae Schoenfeldt; E-Book Builders for Beyond DEF

File version: 201910013.006

BOOKS BY GEORGETTE

Portal City Protectors
Mated to the Capo
Mated to the Enforcer
Mated to the Prince

The Alpha Billion-weres
The Billion-were Needs a Mate
A Cub for the Billion-were
The Billion-were Claims His Mate

Timber Valley Pack
Bride of the Alpha
Purr for the Alpha
Hard as Steele
Lynx on the Loose
Taken by the Alpha
Won't Be Denied

Shifters, Inc.
The Alpha Meets His Match
His Purrfect Mate
Pixie the Lion Tamer
The Bear Who Loved Me
Spotting His Leopard
Blackmailed by the Wolf

Blue Moon Junction
The Alpha Claims a Mate
The Bobcat's Tale
Hard to Bear
My Heart Laid Bear

Starcrossed Dating Agency
The Vulfan's True Mate
The Dragon Claims His Treasure
The Vulfan's Dark Desires

The Mating Game
Big Bad Wolf
Dating a Dragon
A Grizzly Kind of Love

Alpha Prime
Shiftily Ever After
His Curvy Mate

Bridenapped
The Alpha Chronicles
The Alpha's Choice

Shifters of Silver Peak
Mate Marked
Mate for a Month
A Very Shifty Christmas

Tri-Valley Dragon
Bride of the Dragon
Love Burns

Twin Alphas
Claimed
Desired

Neck Deep
Neck Deep in Trouble
Neck Deep in Vampires

Curvy Girls
The Big Girl and the Bounty Hunter
Sweet Surrender
Claimed by the Cowboy

Standalones
I Married a Warlock
Like Cats and Dogs
Lion's Den
The Dragon's Christmas Wish
Shifter's Solace
Furrever Yours

BOOKS BY LETEISHA

Dark Romance

Pinnacle Heirs
(co-authored with Ginger Talbot)
Irrepairable
Cutter
Mangled

Standalones
Whispers in the Dark
Going Under
Vanquished

The Lost Series
One Hour Girl
Scarred
Phenomenal

Paranormal Romance

Portal City Protectors
(co-authored with Georgette St Clair)
Mated to the Capo - St. Clair Only
Mated to the Enforcer
Mated to the Prince
Fated to the Traitor

Single Titles
Claimed Trilogy
Taken Trilogy

Military Romance
A SEALed Fate Series
Protecting Butterfly
Protecting Goddess
Protecting Vixen
Protecting Hawk
Protecting Heartbeat
Corporate Hitman Trilogy

MATED TO THE *PRINCE*

The lions want to kill her ... and then it gets worse ...
  Staying under the radar of the Mage Society's Trinity Council hasn't been much of an issue for bakery owner Kalinda Thorton, but when her supposedly weak magical powers start causing afternoon delights, she knows she's in trouble. Add in one dangerously alluring wolf who says he wants to eat more than just her confections and life in Encantado, Nevada, has gone from enchanted to cursed in one afternoon.

He'll huff and puff and keep his mate safe ...
  Kalinda belongs to the big bad wolf—Romano Moretti. He'll stop at nothing to protect his mate, even if she doesn't yet know they belong together. But clashing with the Trinity Council and a pride of lion shifters at the same time is a lot of work for one wolf, and he might have bitten off more than he can chew.

Kalinda is nobody's witch ...
  Screw the Council, screw the lions, and most especially screw Romano's scorching touch and fierce protection. She'll handle things on her own even if it kills her, except Romano's sizzling embrace makes her yearn for things she's never thought she wanted. She's beginning to wonder if a big bad wolf is exactly the kind of ally she needs, in more ways than one.

With the fate of the town at stake, Kalinda will need to trust someone ... or everyone is doomed.

MATED to the PRINCE

CHAPTER ONE

Giuliana Moretti paced back and forth in Kalinda's living room. Everything inside her was tensed, pulled so tight her bones ached with the strain. It didn't help her Alpha had clipped a leash on his anger only enough to keep the mages in the room from wailing in agony. She was ready to beg on the floor for him to let up the pressure from his power, but pride kept her from saying a thing.

Sometimes it *really* sucked being an Enforcer—a job she always thought she wanted until she got it.

Hindsight, they say, is twenty-twenty.

"On the other side of my gun ..." Dominic repeated the part from Heath's text to Lorenzo for the umpteenth time.

It didn't fail to make her wolf want to blast through her skin this time, as if she'd only heard it once. To threaten one of their people would normally be a death sentence.

But Heath ...

The Lombardi Pack had adopted Lorenzo and Heath, along with Lorenzo's girlfriend Cin, when Dominic mated Zoey. The young teens may not have been a part of the underworld side of things, but they were family. Heath had always been with Cin, and when Lorenzo joined the group, they'd been inseparable.

Sure, things had been a bit weird lately—understatement of the *world*—but all the changes around them would be hard for anyone. Maybe Heath had gotten himself into some trouble and that's why he'd sent that text. She didn't want to believe he was just another blow to them in the short time they'd been a pack.

Giuliana clenched her fists. "Alpha, he is young—"

Dominic whirled to face her, his teeth bared as his deep growl filled the room. "He threatened one of *mine*."

The worst thing anyone could do was to go against an Alpha like Dominic. He was a monster when it came to care for his pack, even when he'd only been *Capo* under Arturo in the Moretti Pack. Taking over the former Bianchi Pack and making it his own had only made him worse.

Not that Giuliana couldn't appreciate him for it. *But still…* "Heath is one of ours."

Silence filled the room as Giuliana stood her ground. Alpha or not, she'd spent more of her life standing toe-to-toe with men like Dominic, and she wasn't going to stop now. He might knock her on her ass, but she'd make sure he'd feel it in the morning.

She'd always been one of them, yet different. The protected princess. The crazy one who snuck out at any time of night and wrecked fucking shop. Teetering between the two sides was enough to give her whiplash.

"Careful, Giuliana."

"*You* be careful. You don't keep me beside you because I kiss your ass."

No, he probably was keeping an eye out for her so she didn't get a hangnail. That's the only reason she'd been able to guess why Arturo had let Dominic take her into his pack in the first place.

Arturo Moretti, the Alpha of the Moretti Pack, didn't give up control lightly. She figured it had a lot more to do with her being a thorn in his side and wanting to pass it to Dominic than thinking it was because he saw her value.

Not that he didn't love her, but an Alpha male's love was … stifling. Giuliana didn't know how Zoey dealt with Dominic regularly, and Kalinda … well, she was lucky her mate wasn't an Alpha. But Romano was Dominic's number two, and if anyone could run the Lombardi Pack when he wasn't there, it was him.

Assholes. She could manage too, if they'd let her.

Dominic glared at Giuliana. "And I'm supposed to … what, ask him nicely why he said what he said?"

"Dom, you know these kids." Lorenzo's face twisted, and Giuliana rolled her eyes. "These *men*. They've been right by our sides and helping out through the Lombardi Community Center. They kept things looking pretty normal while we were all twisted up with Kalinda and the Trinity Council."

"And that's supposed to make me feel differently?"

"No, Alpha, it's supposed to make you think. What could send Heath running off like this?"

Instead of answering her, Dominic looked to Romano. "You have to stay at Kalinda's side. Her position as ruler of the Trinity Council is solidified, but she's got to have a chance to make the changes for Encantado. Zoey has a complication, so I'm here. I don't want to risk the baby letting her use her map magic."

Ohhhhh. You want my foot so far up your ass you won't be able to sit until the second coming.

Giuliana hated to be ignored.

Romano—mate to the newly appointed National Council member Kalinda—smiled. Of course, it wasn't a nice smile. Like, at all. Giuliana was certain Lorenzo was going to puke at the sight of it. Maybe he should, and Giuliana would make sure it landed squarely on said wolf's pretty little shoes.

The young man hunched in his seat and grew pale. "Are you … are you going to kill him?"

That was the twenty-million-dollar question, and Giuliana wasn't so sure Lorenzo wanted to hear the answer.

"If it comes to it."

No filter. No remorse. It was that simple for Dominic.

Giuliana also knew there was only one option for *who* could go. Dominic may be Alpha of the Lombardi Pack, whose numbers weren't as small as they led Encantado to believe, but he still kept those he trusted with internal shit close to the vest.

Before he even opened his mouth to say what she knew was coming, she sighed. "Think Arturo will let me borrow Ciro so I don't have to shut down my shop?"

Ciro was the best scenter for the Moretti Pack. The Lombardi and Moretti had joined in allegiance when Zoey's child was revealed to be a future female Alpha. Because of that, the packs had been helping each other with business the last few months. Ciro's nose also helped her get some prime products for her store, and she trusted him with the inner workings. At least with Ciro around to help her while she was working on this mission, she wouldn't have to stress about it.

Touch of Old—her vintage shop—wasn't about money for her. It was a place she could be herself without the regulations of rules and the walls of protection the men in her life were determined to build around her. Dominic gave her more freedom than her uncle Arturo ever had, but he still kept her close.

Being his Enforcer only meant she could fight for the pack when the time called for it, but he still looked to Romano for the most dangerous work. Mating had only shifted the way Dominic and Romano faced danger.

Or allowed Giuliana to be regarded as more than a healer when shit hit the fan.

"Ciro has already been called in and will be at your store within the hour."

A knock at the door stopped her retort. Probably a good thing because she would have made a scene. They could have at least *acted* like she had a fucking choice.

Hello, right here. Grown-ass woman.

She swore sometimes they were still in the 1600s when women couldn't make their own choices and live like they wanted. But whoever knocked was coming in, and her world shifted.

Mine.

Oh, hell *no. You sit your ass down somewhere.*

His scent hit her first—deep and cool, woods with a touch of snow, fresh game hiding in their dens. Nobody she'd ever met smelled like *him*, and her wolf wanted to roll around in it. Giuliana pressed her fingernails into her palm to clear her head.

Mine.

I said no, you slut.

Talking to her wolf like it was a person was a bad habit. She blamed it on a lifetime of having to befriend herself in a world where anyone could hurt her or betray the pack. Of course, that also made her wolf a hard-headed asshole.

And a repetitive one, apparently.

Mine!

Grrrr.

Everyone disappeared as Pasquale Bianchi came into the room. He stood tall, his head thrown back and shoulders broad enough to take on the world. His dark hair fell over his forehead and covered one eye before he pushed it away.

His body is a wet dream.

In solid black, the t-shirt stretched across his built chest, and his waist tapered into narrow lines where his shirt was tucked into his cargo pants.

"Alpha."

A single word. One that should have been in subjugation when addressing one higher than him. But somehow, Pasquale's call was on equal ground with Dominic. He didn't bend, and he didn't expose his throat.

Power.

She couldn't argue with her wolf on that point. The Bianchi Pack may have been no more, but it was alive within him. Her wolf did that annoying *yip!* of appreciation inside her head, and Giuliana wished she could strangle the beast. She was *not* in the mood for a chance to jump Pasquale's bones. Besides, the man had been driving her wolf fucking batty since he'd arrived on the scene, and Giuliana had been trying hard enough to ignore the rude animal.

I bet his cock is rude too.

Oh, I'm going to kill you, wolf. I swear to fuck.

Admit it ... you thought of it.

She had, and she was more agitated than ever at her wolf's inner thoughts. But ... the man *was* sexy.

Dominic's eyes narrowed, but he didn't reprimand Pasquale on his approach. "You will be with Giuliana. Your only goal is to bring Heath to me."

Excuse me?

Pasquale's gaze touched Giuliana, his nostrils flaring for a moment, and the heat of his attention raked over her body until

5

her nipples hardened to painful peaks. He shook his head. "I can work better on my own. I've tracked Heath out of pack lands."

"I didn't ask. You will work with Giuliana."

Not that she wanted to work with Pasquale either, but what the hell did he mean he worked better alone? Giuliana may have been running a shop now, but she had been in the thick of things since she'd grown up at Arturo's side. Granted, she'd had to sneak out to do it, but who'd been there when Dominic was severely wounded in an explosion? Who got chunks taken out of her hide when they had to bust Kalinda out of the Trinity Council before she took over?

Giuliana, that's who.

Screw him and his high horse if he believed she wasn't good enough.

"The Alpha has demanded my presence."

Pasquale looked back at her, and everything inside her locked up and caught fire. His dark gaze was slow with its perusal of her body, from the top of her sun-kissed hair to the tips of her shit-kicker boots. She wasn't always dressed militant, but she'd been prepared to move on Dominic's order for Heath.

Pasquale's nostrils flared again, and he inhaled deeply, eyes flickering gold for a moment before settling back to bedroom scxcapade instantly. Ignoring Romano and Dominic, he stalked across the room to get up close and personal. His heated breath fanned over her shoulder, sending shock waves pulsing through her system. His lips danced just a hair from her ear, and she trembled.

Open floor and sink inside.

"I can smell your arousal from here, Enforcer. Don't push me on this. Neither of us want what this means."

His words were barely a whisper. Even with their shifter hearing, Dominic and Romano wouldn't have heard him, but she did. It cut. She wasn't sure why, and didn't want to examine it too closely either, but it forced her to suck in a pained breath.

Always, fucking always.

"*Not today, Giuliana.*"
"*Stay where it's safe.*"
"*Just finish the paperwork.*"
"*Heal the wolves.*"
"*One day, I'll match you with a male worthy of you.*"

The last had come from Arturo—a promise of mating that would have enhanced the holding of the pack. She'd always understood that, while they looked like humans, they were wolves at heart—wild and uncontainable—with the added danger of mafia life. Their packs had been bred from Born and Made wolves who grew up in the life and never turned from it.

Giuliana's greatest asset was being a Born wolf with Arturo's blood in her veins. No one cared about her long-dead parents. No one cared about her healing skills. They didn't even care about her quick wit and fighting spirit. It had always been about what she could do.

It fucking sucked to think being with Dominic wouldn't be any different.

In some ways, the man raised as her brother hurt her just as much as everyone else. And now Pasquale added salt to the wound. Giuliana pressed her shoulders back, pushing her breasts against Pasquale's chest, and snarled at him.

"The desire for my wolf to fuck is biological, *Bianchi*. I go where my Alpha tells me to go."

She didn't give a shit about keeping her voice down. When Pasquale snarled, she caught the anger in his gaze before he could mask it. *Fuck. Him.* The Bianchi—more specifically their former Alpha Primo—had attempted to overthrow the Moretti Pack, and their inclusion under Dominic's pack had been a boon from Arturo when the dust settled.

"Are you both finished?"

Giuliana only held Pasquale's gaze a moment longer before looking at Dominic. "We are. We will coordinate and head out. All I ask is that I be given the chance to question Heath."

"Granted. But you'll bring him back here first. If *I* don't like the answers he gives you, I'll take care over."

She nodded. It was the best she was going to get out of him.

"Your place, or mine?" she tossed at Pasquale over her shoulder as she stalked toward the door. She was going to get this right, and she was going to put him in his place too.

"Yours."

His deep-timbred response nearly made her knees weak. It would have really messed her up her bad girl exit by falling out on the floor. Totally.

Mine!

Not if I can help it. I've got toys if this gets too hard for little old you.

I already know what I want to play with.

Ugh. You're an asshole.

He can play with that too.

Giuliana officially hated her wolf more than all the bastards in the room.

CHAPTER *Two*

Giuliana Moretti was the most beautiful woman Pasquale had ever seen—and he'd been surrounded by them all his life. Priceless gems with no voice and even less control over their lives. Under his father, Primo, he'd learned the women were fodder and had seen the worst of what a wolf could be.

Even more so when his own father decided Pasquale wouldn't be given a place as the Alpha's son.

No, that privilege went to his sister, Fabiana, and what she could have created if she'd successfully married Dominic as originally planned. The orchestration had failed, his father left dead, his sister hiding away to lick her wounds, and his former pack split.

Giuliana may have been more than he could ever wish for in a mate, with her outspoken manner and her lush curves, but he couldn't take the chance. He'd lost too much, and he had enough with his wolf to deal with. Mating her would only cause what he'd been keeping under wraps to explode. His packmates needed him to keep his head on straight so they could have a better life than the one they'd had under his abusive Alpha father.

But watching her hips sway as she stomped her way to her car parked out front made Pasquale wish he could follow his wolf's needs.

There was no doubt Giuliana was the wolf fashioned to be the other half of him. It was unfortunate it had to be realized in the fire and snuffed out before either of them had ever had a chance.

Giuliana wrenched open the door of her sedan, and he pressed his lips into a firm line. He didn't like being in vehicles, at all. Too much metal, too cramped and closed in for his wolf to be comfortable. The burn of his wolf pressing against his skin to get out and run free made him hesitate.

Not now.

Giuliana scanned the road in front of Kalinda's home before turning to him. "Where is your car?"

"I didn't drive one."

A sigh met his ears. "Well, get in."

Not going to happen. "I know where you live. I'll meet you there."

"We don't have time for this. You need to catch me up to speed on what you know about Heath before we head out. The sooner the better."

"At best, you live five minutes from your Alpha. I can cover that ground faster than your car."

Pasquale spun around and loped off, ignoring her as she called his name. His legs ate up the distance. He may not have been as fast as his wolf when he wasn't shifted, but he still could challenge a car. He'd always been better, stronger, and smarter than the other wolves around him. He could recognize Dominic for what he was—strong and ruling with an iron fist, tempered with love for his pack. Pasquale could respect the love and how Dominic really cared for the wolves around him. Although Dominic's heritage and the way he'd become a wolf had created something in him that should have been impossible, he was not Pasquale.

He was not a Born wolf meant to be Alpha from his first cry. He was not a pup able to tackle wolves twice his age. He'd never been trained to face fears and overcome them, despite them threatening to break him.

But Pasquale had.

In some ways, Pasquale was more wolf than Dominic ever hoped to be, and more *Capo* as well. Understanding that, however, didn't change reality—Dominic *was* the head of Lombardi Pack,

Bianchi was no more, and Pasquale's place was precarious at best. If it wasn't for his nose and the skills he had in combat, he was sure he wouldn't be as involved in the inner workings of Lombardi as he was.

He pressed harder, working his legs faster. The burn helped clear his mind and singed away the bitter taste of pissed-away loss he couldn't recoup. He'd have enough to face with finding Heath … and finding the missing wolves who'd once been with Bianchi. Not all of them had come with the roll-in under Dominic, and it worried Pasquale.

"You don't like cars."

He slid to a stop. Giuliana was right beside him, close enough he should have known she was there. Close enough that her citrus and heated scent filled his nose. It was her, femininity hidden behind power. Her glittering gaze zeroed in on him, and she saw too much.

He rolled his shoulders. "What?"

"You don't like cars."

"Why do you say that?"

She narrowed her eyes before nodding her head at her front door. Her car was nowhere to be seen.

She ran with me. How did she keep up?

Confused, and more than a little intrigued, he followed her up on to her porch covered in green plants. He bit back a groan as she caressed a broad leaf on a tree.

Mine.

I know, but we can't have her.

Says who?

Me.

Pfft. I run the show.

See when's the next time I let you go racing after bunnies. Who's the bitch now?

His wolf growled at him, but he ignored the beast. They'd been having this argument for months since coming to this pack, and Pasquale wasn't in the mood to start it up again. He only focused on following Giuliana into her home.

It was warm and vibrant, all colors and soft pillows. She's created something more of a den, with an open floor plan where he could see her entire space. Her living room flowed into her dining room and kitchen. Farther back, she had a large bedroom with a low-slung platform bed. He'd never seen a place set up quite like hers. Clothes were neatly hung on poles connected to the wall, like racks at a clothing store, and her shower was surrounded in glass. He figured the toilet had to be in a closed-off space. From anywhere in her home, she could see clear to the other side.

"Do you feel okay in here?"

Pulled from studying her home, he blinked and faced her. She stood in the center of her living room, hands up and palms out, like she was soothing him. He frowned. What the hell was she doing?

"What are you talking about?"

She stepped closer and lifted her hands higher. "Just be calm."

Okay, maybe he needed to reevaluate how perfect she was. Giuliana was acting like a loon, advancing on him in stilted, slow movements. She kept her gaze on his, but he saw the way she slightly tilted her head, the subtle message of submission.

It ... fucked up his world.

The soft slope of her neck, the gentle pulse throbbing, the way she moved. Pasquale's wolf thrashed against his ribcage, howling his need and desire. With each step she took, her scent wrapped around him, sliding over his skin.

When she got close, she pressed her body to him, and he had to clench his fists to stop himself from bending her over the nearest surface and taking her.

"I'm going to take your hand, okay?"

She could take whatever the fuck she wanted. Her hand was so hot as she lifted their joined hands toward his face.

"Come on, big boy."

He growled, and she growled back.

Fuck.

"I'm not the one about to go crazy. Now, stop being an asshole and let me help you."

His wolf wanted to take a nip out of her hide for the disrespect, but at the same time, it loved the fact she'd done it.

Confused bastard.

Speak for yourself.

But when his fingers touched his face, he sucked in a breath. He'd partially shifted. His muzzle elongated, hair had burst out and spread across his face.

"It's been happening ever since I told you to get in the car." She wrapped her other arm around his waist and rested her head on his chest.

Giuliana was not a short woman by any means, but next to his height, she was small. He inhaled her scent deep into his lungs and held his breath.

"You shouldn't be so close like this," he forced himself to say. He wanted her right the fuck where she was, and closer still. But his wolf was losing his mind, and he could smell her arousal on the air.

"Sometimes, when Dominic—"

"I would hope you are *not* about to tell me you do this for him," he growled. He sounded like a jealous man. He wasn't ... right?

She curled her fingers against his chest, digging her nails in enough to sting. A warning. *She* was warning *him*.

Okay, that's not hot at all—

Pfft!

Did his wolf just *pfft* him?

"Interrupting a lady is rude. As I was saying, when Dominic gets like this, Zoey helps. Her touch seems to make it better." Giuliana pulled back and looked over his face. "I guess I can do that for you too."

Pasquale touched his muzzle. His lips were back to normal, his skin smooth. While his wolf was pressing to come out, it was so he could have the woman in front of him instead of the fear of closed-in spaces.

He nodded. "Yes."

Giuliana sighed, tracing some shape on his chest. "It took me years to get used to cars. My need to escape sometimes drove me to conquer it. But many wolves can't be in them."

Her quiet understanding without ridicule was new to him. Pasquale's father had always told him he was weak for not being able to stomach the inside of a car. Of all the fears his father had drilled out of him, claustrophobia was not one of them.

He'd soothed himself by thinking it was because he was more wolf than his father. Because he was more tied to the earth, he couldn't be as human. Pasquale still viewed it as a failure. A history of being the shield when he should have been the crown had taught him to think that way.

Pasquale took a step back, severing the connection with Giuliana. He needed to keep his head clear. Allowing himself her comfort would only bring out more urge to claim her.

Take her.

No. I can't.

Oh, you can. *You just* won't.

Same thing right now. Shut up. I'm thinking.

Being with her, allowing his wolf to rule, would only mean he'd have to destroy her life. He couldn't do it. Not to her.

Giuliana sighed, but Pasquale shook his head, stopping her from saying anything. "Thank you for helping me."

Giuliana crossed her arms over her chest, lifting her breasts for his inspection. She probably didn't mean the move like that, but it made his mouth salivate all the same.

"Let's just put it out there. Our wolves recognize each other as mates."

Hearing the word on her tongue made him tremble. Him, one of the deadliest wolves in Encantado.

"Yes," he answered.

"But neither of us want to claim the other."

"Correct again."

She swallowed, and he could detect … pain. As a scenter, he was aware of subtleties most wolves could only dream of. For those with his skill, they could get information on the wind from miles around. Pasquale could double that, easily. The slightly metallic-tinged scent was similar to a physical wound, but less heated.

He may not be able to claim his mate, but he wouldn't abide her being hurt.

Pasquale closed the distance between them and slid his fingers into the cool thickness of her hair. He gripped the strands, forcing her head back so she had to look at him. Her eyes widened, and fear danced in her gaze. And there it was—part of why he could never take her.

She feared control, capture, dominance.

"I *want* my mate. I'd love nothing more than to taste every part of you, make you mine. Make your knees weak with pleasure. Make sure your body will only want mine for the rest of your days."

He pulled her closer, his mouth hovering just a hair's breadth from hers. He wanted her hot, not afraid. Never of him. "Don't think, for a moment, I deny you because you aren't everything I could want in a mate. Don't think I don't fight my wolf at every step. I've been here long enough to see the sort of woman you are, Giuliana. But my wolf … wants things you can't accept. Needs what would only send you running."

It was more than that, but he couldn't explain it. Couldn't share what he knew in his heart. The Lombardi Pack didn't know the dynamic of the Bianchi. Didn't know he was Primo's son. Didn't know he'd been meant to be Alpha. The wildness of Kalinda's rise to the Trinity Council, Zoey's pregnancy, Silva living among them—a Fae Queen—and attacks on Encantado probably helped to keep his secret under wraps. To help, he never shifted around them, never let the power rise to the surface.

Claiming Giuliana would force him to.

There couldn't be two Alphas in a pack for long, and Pasquale had a kingdom in shambles.

Let them believe he was only a scenter and Fabiana was the chosen one. It was safer that way. If he had to lose his mate to keep his pack with a home and safety, he'd do so.

They'd been hurt enough.

Giuliana needed freedom as much as he needed control. Their lives had ruined what they could have been.

"We aren't saying no to each other because the other is lacking."

It was a statement, but he heard the question in it. She was asking, more than anything, if he was saying no to her because he found her less than what he wanted. For a moment, just a moment, he would be her mate.

For a few heartbeats, he wouldn't be so alone in the world.

He crashed his lips to hers.

CHAPTER THREE

Pasquale's mouth was burning silk and bite. Giuliana had never been kissed like this.

There was mastery in his touch, command, as he used her hair to turn her head and fit their mouths together. The way he guided her was wild. His tongue danced over hers, a broad stroke of fire blazing over her nerve endings. But it wasn't just her mouth. Pasquale stayed a rock, hard and unforgiving, and raked her over him. He used his free arm to warp around her waist and push and pull her body against him from side to side. It caused a delicious friction across her nipples and rubbed her stomach against the hard plane of his abs.

Giuliana was swaying, wrapped up in his embrace and his absolute demand of her movements. He gifted her with his kiss and forced her to experience every nuance.

He broke their lips apart, and she lurched forward, following his deadly touch. His fist in her hair stopped her short, pain pricking her scalp and fanning the fire.

"Have you ever come from a kiss, *bella*?"

Beautiful. *He called me beautiful.*

She shook her head, and he smiled. The cocksure, half-twisted grin changed his features. It was playful and daring at the same time.

"I'll ask you that again in a little bit."

Mine!

Yes, for right now, so let's enjoy this.
So pretty.
Agreed.

Pasquale took her mouth once more, but this time he used his other hand to grip her throat. The threat of his power rolled over her, making her tense. His fingertips soothed for a moment, rubbing their way over her pulse until she melted back into his touch.

Won't hurt you.

The thought flittered through her mind just as he lifted her off the floor by her neck and stalked to her dining room table. He placed her on the tabletop, never releasing his hold, and devoured her.

She panted, trying to keep up, as her nipples hardened to the point of pain and her stomach clenched.

"Open your eyes. Don't look away."

A demand. One she couldn't ignore. She forced her eyes open and met Pasquale's much darker ones. An edge of gold around the rim made her suck in a breath.

What—

He didn't let her finish the thought. Power wrapped around her, licking its way over her skin. Her clothes didn't matter; there was no barrier any longer. She moaned into Pasquale's mouth, sucking on his tongue. Her hips jerked, craving friction, and he gave it to her. He gave her everything she ever could have wanted. Similar to Dominic's Alpha call but softened to a brilliant edged blade, Pasquale's call sliced through her fear, through her need to break free. All that was left was Giuliana—without the history, without the need to fight back. She could flow, basking in him, without the baggage of the years.

Tears pooled in her gaze.

She didn't recognize that woman, didn't know who she was anymore. But Pasquale saw it; his studying gaze missed nothing.

He pressed his power closer, sliding down over her collarbone to her breasts. Phantom tongues licked across her nipples, rough, making her jerk. Pasquale mirrored it in the kiss, tasting his way along her sensitive gums above her canines. They exploded in her mouth, giving a dangerous edge to their embrace.

Giuliana caught her breath, holding on, waiting, and Pasquale was there, spreading his touch across her stomach and down under her pants to her pussy. A hot, fierce swath of force worked her clit.

Pasquale was everywhere. Her mouth, her breasts, between her legs. They all worked together, sending waves of heated pleasure through her. It rolled, crashing against her with more force, making her thighs clench around his waist. She gripped his shirt, using him as an anchor in the maelstrom.

Wetness slicked the insides of her thighs, and she rolled her hips. Each rock brought her closer to the edge, each a new bite of zinging force. She throbbed with it, and it swelled from her groin and up through her body.

Yes!

She leaned back, bracing her hands on the table. Pasquale never broke the kiss, and she trusted him to hold them as she lost herself. The new position allowed her to move more freely, riding his power like she wanted to ride him. She took, claiming her needs, begging for more. Pasquale met her, adding more force, more touch.

Giuliana couldn't hope to best him, to ask for more than he could give. Without a doubt, she knew he could do this without touching her at all. That he could leave her a pile of undulating mess on her table over and over again.

Her soul jerked, her wolf howling, her eyes watering with strain. It couldn't be tears. It couldn't be. But Pasquale knew better. His thumb caressed over her cheek, soaking away the moisture, and she came undone. That singular, soft touch, blew her apart.

She screamed into his mouth, her world darkening until only his face remained. He furrowed her brows, his eyes half-open as pain spread across his features.

He's going to let go.

She knew it and understood. But in the wake of what they could be, it only made her cry harder. The woman who never cried, who never let herself look weak. He'd broken her without even trying, and part of her hated that they had seen this side of mating.

That they'd even tested it.

There was nowhere to escape, nowhere to run, and for the first time, she wished her space had a closed room where she could hide. Instead, she let the kiss break and faced Pasquale. He was swollen and stiff between her legs, and she realized he hadn't attempted to take his own pleasure.

When was the last time someone had taken care of *her*?

When was the last time she could remember not having to fight for what *she* wanted?

He framed her face with his large, calloused hands and thumbed away her tears as fast as they fell. "Do you see now?"

"That was ... Alpha—"

He shook his head. "I'm no Alpha."

But he was. She'd tasted it, knew it. And with that came another realization. He couldn't claim a mate without his power coming out. He'd be forced to. A wolf's mating called up every instinct they had, switched their allegiance to their mate first. She was Dominic's Enforcer now that Romano was his *Capo*. If her Alpha wanted to punish her, Pasquale would attack. Every instinct within him would be focused on protecting her.

And she'd learned long ago what an Alpha's protection was.

Of course, The Fates—those bitches—would give her a mate who was everything she wanted to get away from. Life had taught her men held on too tightly and confused love with near obsession of safety and care.

No, she couldn't have that. Never. She needed to be free, needed to live her own life and make her own choices. She wouldn't be able to do that with Pasquale. He'd made his point clear in ways he couldn't imagine.

It wasn't about wanting each other. It was more about the fundamental difference in their wolves. Perhaps, if she had met him before, things would be different. She could appreciate that he understood, that he saw what others around her didn't, and was letting her be.

Just sucked it had to be her mate.

"You may not be a recognized Alpha, Pasquale, but no wolf can do what you just did if they weren't Alpha."

He shrugged, but it was pained. "I know, but who I am doesn't matter. There've been too many changes lately. Maybe if things had been ..." He let his words trail off and shook his head. "It doesn't matter. Things are the way they are, and we have a pack member to find. This thing between us will only make things messy. Focusing on the job at hand is better all the way around."

Maybe it was because she still had subtle explosion rocking between her legs. Maybe it was because she wanted to taste his mouth once more. Or maybe it was just because she was used to fighting against men who seemed to have her best interests at heart, but it only happened to satisfy them. Whatever the reason, Giuliana didn't let it go.

"So you're deciding *for* me?"

He frowned. "You don't want this mating."

"I am so *sick* of everyone telling me what I can and can't do. It's *my* life."

"You said it yourself, Giuliana."

"Um, yeah, before you went exce-fucking-llent between my legs with the juju works. I should have the choice to have more of that if I want it."

"Exce-fucking-llent juju works?"

He smiled again, and it stopped her heart just like it had the first time. She *liked* him, or at least the small hints of who he was that peeked out when he didn't have to hide it. She wanted to know more of that side of him.

You want his cock.

That too.

Mine!

Let's not get carried away. I just want to jump his bones when I want to.

Mine!

Okay, you're turning into an annoying bitch, and I don't like it.

Technically, I am a bitch, by definition.

I hate you.

Love you too.

Irritation at her wolf notwithstanding, it was still true. She just wanted the choice. That's all.

Pasquale watched her for a moment. "Do you always make faces when you talk to your wolf?"

"She can be annoying."

"Don't I know it."

"Your wolf talks back to you too?"

"Presently he's telling me to bend you over, and I'm trying to explain to him the intricacies of human affairs."

"How's that going for you?"

"He's feigning snoring at the moment."

She blinked. "You talk to your wolf like it's a person too?"

Pasquale's ears went pink. Most wolves, from what she'd learned, communicated with their wolf in single words or reactions from the wolf only. It wasn't typical to have conversations. Yell in a losing battle against a stubborn wolf, yes, but not actually talk to them. She'd never met anyone else who could.

"He's my best friend."

The sentence was low, but she heard it. Heard the story behind the words, even if she didn't know the details. Loneliness, separation, pain. The same reasons she'd created such a bond with her wolf too.

Giuliana slid off the table and stayed still long enough to make sure her knees wouldn't play hokey pokey and turn themselves around before she lifted her chin.

"How about this … We let this happen."

"Come again."

She rolled her eyes even as her thighs clenched. *Cheeky bastard.* She motioned between them. "This thing between us."

He looked down his body at the raging hard-on between his legs. "It *is* still between us."

He had jokes. This stoic, quiet man who was always silent except to address the danger of a situation, had jokes.

She liked that too, and even more so because she was the only one really seeing it.

"Mating."

At that, he clammed up. "No."

"I don't mean right now, as it may never happen, but we don't have to walk around each other like we don't know what's going on."

"I thought that's what we just established. We know we want each other, but we know we can't."

"And I'm saying we've probably let life make too many decisions for us. We won't seek it out, but if it happens, it happens."

His eyes glittered for a moment, and she sucked in a breath. "There is no 'if' with my wolf. If I let myself go, I *will* claim you."

Okay, I can also add loving when he goes growly to the sexy list.

"Why are you being so difficult?"

"I'm just being honest, *bella*. I take what I want."

"And I'd fight you if it's not something I want to give."

They glared at each other, two strong souls clashing without moving a muscle. A battle of wills and intent. He may be strong enough to be an Alpha, but she was the niece of one and the Enforcer of another.

In essence, no punk bitch. Snort. Bitch.
Don't start, wolf.
I finished already, thank you.

Said wolf flicked her tail, showing her ass, and stalked off.

Sometimes Giuliana wished she could strangle her.

You're messing up my badass moment.

There was no reply, of course, and Giuliana shook her head.

"We find Heath, and if things happen, we take the battle when it comes. Deal?"

Pasquale only stared before he shook. Everything … changed. He grew larger—it was the only way she could describe it. His essence swelled, making his shoulders impossibly broad, his legs strong as oak trees, and his head cocked to the side. The press of his power nearly forced her to her knees, and she had to fight to keep on her feet. Canines burst forth in his mouth. Hers did the same in response.

"Be sure of your choice. It could mess up everything in our lives. It could mean losing your pack … again. It would mean learning things that could change everything you ever thought you knew. I am not a man to be played with, Giuliana. If I become serious about claiming you, there is nowhere you can run."

She swallowed against his threat, knowing he was giving her the last chance.

But he'd sealed his fate. He did the one thing no one else had ever fucking done.

He gave her the *choice*.

"Deal. So when do we leave to go after Heath?"

CHAPTER *Four*

"I've tracked Heath out of Lombardi Pack lands."

"I knew that. So why does that sound like a death toll now?"

They hadn't left immediately after her declaration of war. And it *was* a war. Pasquale had closed in on himself, probably arguing with his wolf even as Giuliana did a celebratory dance with hers. It wasn't a mating or anything yet. That wasn't what they'd agreed on, but it could most definitely be the end result. The whole thing made Giuliana itch, but she couldn't deny the way they came together was electrifying.

Even beyond climax-of-the-century addled brain, she could see how they could work … maybe. But it was nice to allow things to just go without a definite choice from the outset. The sequence of events was enough to make her feel like she'd been tossed up in a tornado, but at least she had some control now and that put her back on solid ground.

Pasquale's hesitance to tell her about Heath worried her though. She didn't want the young man to die because he'd made a stupid mistake, but even she couldn't change things if he'd made too many. She looked to Pasquale to clarify how fucked they were.

Not enough.

Shut up, wolf!

"It's in the direction of Scorched Earth."

Holy. Shit.

Scorched Earth was an example of how dangerous portal cities could be. While each had their own breed of shifters and paranorms that lived alongside mages, they consistently weren't all gold and glittery. Encantado was known for their wolves, with only a small group of lions—now even less—and phoenix shifters. They also housed some daywalkers, but mages held the largest number. The mages couldn't stand against the shifters if things went south because, while they had numbers, they didn't have many battle capable mages of high level.

Scorched Earth was one place all sides feared. Closest to the portal out, it was protected heavily by shifters and mages alike in case another monstrosity wanted to come through to destroy. The name came from the destructive damage a wayward dragon had created before it was annihilated. It was twenty square miles of charred land many only went near to sightsee.

"Why would he go there? Heath grew up on the streets of District 17. He knows the ropes better than any of us."

"No one guards Scorched Earth from people going in. Their eyes are only on the portal itself and the area surrounding Customs when people come in from the outside. Too much land to cover."

"It's a death sentence there. Nothing grows, no amenities. Nothing. Why run there?"

"I don't know. But he didn't travel down south where the Moonstone Pack runs the entertainment section, nor is he close to Trinity Council lands."

"You've been busy."

"The moment Kalinda alerted me of a missing pack member, I went searching before clues got lost. I could only travel so far before being summoned, but I know our heading."

"He bypassed Greenwald Park."

Greenwald was a wolf's dream. Filled with trees, it had open space to run and ran from the west to east side of Encantado. It served as a barrier as well, standing between Moretti and Lombardi Lands and the side of Encantado typically reserved for upper-class mages. They resided near the more touristy location of the south. They didn't mind being so close to the more cultured southern wolves. It would have been easier to disappear in Greenwald.

Pasquale nodded. "I would have done the same thing too."

"Why?"

"Because you don't go where anyone would be fine to follow you."

Giuliana paced in her living room. "Then you feel like he left on his own choice."

"I never believed he left under any other way. The reason may be unknown, but that doesn't change what happened. The why isn't something we can deal with until we know more or find him."

"Agreed. So how are we going to do this?"

"We're going to follow the trail, that's how."

It made sense to him, of course. For her, she'd only seen scenters work from afar. They typically stayed to themselves, their nose giving them more information than others were willing to share. And other times, their nose could be what hurt them. Ciro, for example, could handle being in her shop with her old stuff because she kept it spotless and free from dust. But when she first opened, he couldn't walk in without going into sneezing fits.

Pasquale stayed away from the inner circle's mated pairs unless called. Giuliana wondered if it messed with his nose like Ciro's.

First, she needed to understand what "following the trail" actually meant.

She sighed and leaned against the wall. "Explain for the non-scenter in the room because that just sounded like a cheesy cop line."

Pasquale chuckled, and her lady bits started acting stupid. Was *everything* about him supposed to make her want to jump him?

Um, yes. Mate. Hellloooo.

What if I shift underwater next time?

You wouldn't.

Try me.

"Sorry. Old habits die hard. We're going to pack light for several days and travel on foot to follow where the scent leads. Once we find him, we can call in for pickup, but it's easier and less obvious if we travel through Greenwald as our wolves until we reach Scorched Earth."

"Weapons?"

He frowned at her. "We're wolves."

Giuliana rolled her eyes. "Yeah, I know. But we're still expected to work with the Family. If we reach Scorched Earth without some appearance of our business, they'll wonder what's up. The shifters there on guard would think we're deserting our pack or up to some shit."

"Are the border lands so harsh?"

It was her turn to frown at him. "Have you ever been? Of course, they're like that. Being caught there without authorization is the same as leaving a pack. It's not that leaving a pack is wrong, but trying to run from a portal city is illegal."

"Politics." He turned the word to a harsh curse.

"Yes, but belonging to a pack with grease all over the place could help. No one will question why wolves from the Lombardi Pack are in Scorched Earth."

"The pack's that strong?"

"Yes and no. The alliance with Moretti has strengthened us, and now there is Kalinda …"

She let her words trail off. Okay, so she was entertaining *possibly* having a mating with him and dealing with him long enough not to want to rip his head off, but she was still an Enforcer for Dominic. That meant other than what may be common knowledge, she wasn't going to share what Dominic had not.

For all intents and purposes, Pasquale was not even a ranking member of Lombardi while he was still establishing his loyalty. Technically, in the pecking order, she outranked him.

The Morettis and Bianchis never got along. The battle between Primo and Arturo expanded into even their *Capos* and brewed under the surface for years. Arturo had changed his cousins Ottavio and Carlo in the 1950s. Unfortunately, only Carlo appreciated it. Ottavio's aggravation with Arturo's accumulation of wealth and power made him jealous. Enough to plan a coup with the Bianchi Pack, while also positioning Primo's daughter, Fabiana, in a prime location at Dominic's side.

Had they succeeded, Arturo would have been dead, and they would have had a Bianchi in place over the Moretti Pack as well as increasing their own. Giuliana had lived with it, watching Dominic struggle to handle the expectations on his shoulders even when he met Zoey, the mate of his heart.

As a scenter, Pasquale should have known much more about the workings of Encantado as a whole, especially a place as big as Scorched Earth. How sheltered and controlled had Primo kept his pack? Hell, Fabiana stayed in the house on the outskirts of Lombardi lands with some of the other former Bianchi members. Giuliana had barely seen the girl except in flashes.

Probably didn't help she'd tried to take Zoey's man.

Kalinda still wanted to punch her for that one.

But they all felt sorry for her too. Giuliana was getting a better picture of how their life may have been.

Pasquale was making faces, and she smiled inside, wondering if he was talking to his wolf too. It was small, but important at the same time.

"Hey," she called.

He shook his head and gave her his attention again. "Yeah?"

"How about this? You teach me about being a scenter, and I'll cover the blanks you may have with the politics of the world."

"We seem to be making a lot of deals lately."

"I'm learning you're not all that you see too. I was taught to hate you based on your name. And I'm sure your pack never cared for the Morettis."

He didn't have to answer her; it was written clearly all over her face. Primo and his *Capo* Luigi had so much to answer for. Too late, as they'd already been removed from the face of the planet, but the hell they'd begun still left ripple effects through them all.

"There are … things I don't want to speak about. Not yet."

She could understand that too. Plenty of her life wasn't ready to be an open book, and her allegiance was—and would always be—with Arturo and Dominic. "We'll figure it out along the way."

"I'm not good with this."

"What? Talking?"

"Sharing."

Pasquale sat on her couch and leaned back, tucking his hands behind his head. That was … sexy. To distract herself, Giuliana sat across from him, feet wide apart and elbows on her knees. Dominic called it her "power sit" right around the time she did it in a Louis Vuitton dress and heels. She didn't care how it looked to others, how they didn't view her as feminine. They needed to see her strength. That she was one of them and not an outsider.

Pasquale sat forward, mirroring her, and the effect was different. All his attention was on her—a single-minded focus she could envy. He placed one fist into the palm of his other hand and waited. In the silence of the room, they stared, two enemies on opposite sides who were forced together by their biology. At least that's how she should have felt.

"Why do you do that?"

She cocked her head to the side. "Do what?"

"Act like a man."

She scoffed. "I'm sure you realize I'm all woman."

His heated gaze made her choke on her attempt at a joke. "Yes, I'm well aware."

"Then what are you asking?"

"You can be decked out in priceless jewels and expensive clothing, yet you staunchly try to push away your femininity."

"I do not."

Of course, Giuliana ruined that argument by jutting her chin forward and glaring at him with all intents to punch him.

He was right; she just wasn't going to talk to him about it. "You don't share, so neither do I."

"Let's add to our deal."

"What's that?"

"You teach me about the world and yourself, and I'll teach you about sniffing and myself too."

Yeah, not going to happen, even if she was really interested in learning more about him. Her wounds were hers, thank you very much, and she'd like to keep them where they were. She was fine with trading explosive orgasms back and forth, not so much on the world of opening up.

"Maybe I'm not good with this either."

Pasquale only nodded. "Challenge accepted."

"It wasn't a challenge."

He ignored her. "Pack what you need, and I'll head back to my house and do the same. I'll meet you back here in an hour."

She *hated* being ignored.

"Did you hear what I said?"

He stood instead of answering her and stretched. Joints popped and realigned as he elongated his powerful frame.

Is my mouth watering? No, must be preparation for vomit.

You lie to yourself so well.

Can it, dog.

I know you are, but what am I?

Ugh.

Still, Pasquale didn't say a word. She stared at him incredulously as he walked to her front door.

"Pasquale."

He stopped and slowly looked at her over his shoulder.

"I don't like to be ignored."

"So you *can* do it."

"What?"

He smiled. "Share."

He was out the door before the table she picked up shattered against the wall where his head would have been.

Careful. Wouldn't want a splinter.

"Oh, would you shut up already?" Now that she was alone, she'd answer her wolf like she usually did.

Nope.

"I didn't share anything!"

Why are you yelling at me? Sharing is caring.

"I didn't share!"

Nothing …

Great. Her wolf was ignoring her too.

CHAPTER FIVE

"Brother."

Pasquale closed his eyes before he shut his front door behind him. Fabiana stood at the bottom of his stairs, her dark hair flowing around her face and down to her hips. Her eyes were haunted and fearful.

Days and weeks may have passed since so much in their life had changed, but Fabiana was still a hiding, broken child. The vixen she'd once been was nothing more than a façade carefully crafted by their father to attract the sort of man he'd believed Dominic to be.

But here—in soft yoga pants and a t-shirt she probably took from his closet and her feet bare—she was nothing more than a woman who still didn't know who she was.

"You can't call me that."

Tears pooled in her eyes. "But that's what you are. We never could say it when … Primo was alive."

Yes. Something else that man would never truly answer for. Fabiana was five years younger. Not much by shifter standards, but she'd be denied having the connection of a protective older brother. She'd been bred and taught to be the future *Capo* wife Primo intended, nothing more or less. If she hadn't overheard an argument between Primo and Pasquale, she wouldn't even know they were related.

"Come here, *cucciola*."

At the familiar nickname, Fabiana brightened. He'd called her "puppy" from the time she was a small child, tripping as she ran behind him. She'd been clumsy and gangly but filled with so much expression.

Their father had ironed that out soon enough. Pasquale wished she remembered how to laugh easily like she did when she was younger. She was small in his arms, so different than Giuliana's vibrance and strength. Fabiana's shoulders had carried too much weight—they curved in on themselves. He pulled her close, inhaling the soft powder and snow of her scent.

The snow ... it came from their mother, born in the mountains. It marked them, reminded them of their bond. Bringing Fabiana into the world had taken their mother's life. Pasquale wished he could blame their mother's death for the change in their father, but he'd been mean and cruel long before Luciana Orneti had taken her last breath.

Their arranged marriage had been doomed from the get-go, and it was why Primo saw nothing wrong with arranging Fabiana's life as well and not waiting for a mate to her wolf.

"What did you do today?"

Fabiana chuckled, a sound like silver bells on the wind. "Why do you ask that all the time?"

"Because I'm interested."

"No one's interested."

He lifted her chin so he could look down at her. "I am not our father. Tell me."

"I painted for a while. But I don't have the right tone to get it done. The one I have is more ultramarine when I want Phthalo blue."

He had no idea what the hell she was talking about. Colors were just that. Why make up such crazy damn names? What the hell was Phthalo blue?

A blue you don't know. Obviously.
You're feeling uppity today, wolf.
No, I was up *earlier, and you left the house.*
She isn't ready.
Ix-nay on the upid-stay.

He rolled his eyes instead of answering the animal inside him. Fabiana caught the eye roll and shrank.

"I'm-I'm sorry."

"It's not you. I'm fussing with Stupid right now."

Fabiana cocked her head to the side. He remembered when she'd done that as a little girl, always studying, always watchful. He wondered for the umpteenth time if she'd have been a scientist or something if they'd left her alone.

"I think you are closer to your animal than most." Her voice was stronger. It did this when she warmed to a topic and didn't have to fear rejection.

Feeling better that he'd gotten a good subject change, he pinched her chin and stepped back.

"You said that before."

She followed him as he went farther into his house. Fabiana's home was for show, at best. Most of the younger pups used her place to hide and practice shifting at rapid speeds. Pasquale's home had become her haven where people knew not to search for her.

And they kept it secret from the Lombardis as well.

"I think the more I think about it, it isn't just about your interaction. Your wolf sounds almost human?"

Pfft. I have four legs, which is better than your stupid two. And I can lick my balls when I want to.

Pasquale choked on a laugh. "Yeah, he does."

"But it's not just what you'd think you'd say, or your tone, right?"

Pasquale nodded. His bedroom was cool and dark, the bed low to the floor just like he liked it.

Of course that made him think of Giuliana's bedroom and what he'd like to do to her in it.

He groaned and focused on his sister's question while packing his go bag. "Yes. His voice is … deeper than mine and doesn't have the same cadence. His thoughts are like mine, yes, but not exactly what I'd say at the time."

At first, he'd thought he was just going crazy, using the wolf as a way to get some separation from the world he was in. That he'd spent so much time talking to himself, he'd created an alter that just sounded like a wolf. But even when he shifted, he noticed his wolf thought the same way, played pranks on him—like tripping up his feet when he was trying to catch a rabbit.

They'd bonded as two souls inhabiting one body instead of just one who was both animal and man. And yet they were one. He couldn't be separated without the other.

"Has he ever taken over control?"

"Like a feral wolf? Of course not."

Some shifters who'd lost their way or sank too much into their misery could shift into their wolf and stay. The longer they stayed in wolf form, the less human they seemed to become. While they were more intelligent, they still appeared to be a wolf.

"Not feral, but he just has the reins."

Can you?

I could, but I won't.

Why?

Because we are one.

So it's about respect.

Yes, but it's also about being trapped.

You'd turn feral.

Yes. And I won't do that to you.

"Were you asking him?"

"Yes. He says he could, but he wouldn't because he could turn feral."

Fabiana tapped her lip, so many thoughts racing through her eyes he couldn't keep up. "I wonder."

He didn't even respond; she was gone anyway. One moment she was a battered shell, unsure of what or who she was, and the next she was in search of answers to questions no one would think to ask. He was happy as long as she became comfortable in her own skin. It might be like walking through a minefield sometimes, but she was worth it.

She deserved to have some peace, and he'd do everything he could to give it to her.

Bag packed, complete with his gun and holster, he clipped the bag on his back, balancing the band that held it over one shoulder and across his chest to the other side of his body. The design allowed for him to shift in and out without being strangled or tied up in something around his front two legs. He'd perfected the art of rolling several sets of clothes into the bag with provisions, water, extra ammo, and a medical kit. He could stay away from his pack for weeks if need be.

Of course, living with the Lombardi Pack almost made it obsolete. Even outside of pack lands, just being within their territory meant he could go to anyone for help. First, that was from fear, but with the work Dominic and Zoey had done, there was respect and care from the people of District 17.

Many still feared the Lombardis, however. For all Zoey's niceness, the wolves had not given up their place as members of the Family. There were still collections, no-holds-barred fights, magic shows, and a casino in the Arena that all brought in money that, sometimes, had bloodstains on it. They hadn't stopped being what others should fear. They'd simply become the monsters who fought for those they loved, and the loved ones didn't view them as enemies.

Evil is always in the eye of the wronged.

He sighed.

Guns always made him think this way, made him remember his training and his skillset.

What his father had bred him to be.

Before he could take one fucking step out of his room, another, more deadly reminder of who he was flashed in the corner of his eye.

Built for wear and accuracy, painstakingly wrapped in bronzed PVD finish along the muzzle and deep brown over the handle, his SIG 1911 Scorpion was a masterpiece in death and destruction. A lifetime of blood and beauty.

We are animals, and I don't mean the wolf within us, Pasquale. Men are the beast. Our claws and our teeth are blades and bullets. Our strategy is the mob mentality. And we live and die by the Law. The fact we are wolves only means we have more in our arsenal. We rule them all.

That was what his father believed, and for a time, he did as well.

Until Primo died.

Until he realized his whole life had been a lie to propel his father's vision.

Still, he reached for the gun. Felt the sense of calm control wrapping around him as he strapped it to his thigh.

Quick release, sight, breathe, shoot.

"Have you told them?"

Fabiana stood before him, papers in her hands. Knowing her, they were notes about his wolf. Thoughts in ink she'd never been allowed to voice before.

"About me? No. It doesn't matter."

"You were not meant to follow another Alpha, Paz."

Calling him by his childhood nickname wasn't going to make him agree with her. "Our people have been through enough. They'd look to me to be like my father, and I'm not him."

"They look to you to protect them, as you always have, when you could. They knew you and love you. We can't stay here."

No, they couldn't. But now …

He couldn't talk to Fabiana about Giuliana. There was still bad blood between the two of them because of Fabiana's part in the hell orchestrated by their father. The pack may have been accepted, but that didn't mean the memory didn't still burn hot. It wasn't the time to open things up, and he wasn't even sure if he'd have a mate when this was all said and done.

All he could do was focus on finding Heath.

"We'll deal with it later. Right now, I've got to head out and find a missing pack member. It's my job."

Fabiana nodded, running one hand down his arm as he passed her. "Come back in one piece."

"Hey, it was one time I came back in a couple pieces."

"No, Paz, you came back *missing* a few pieces. Out of your thigh, if I remember right."

"Toe-may-to, toe-mah-to."

Fabiana rolled her eyes. "Pea-can, puh-con."

"No," he argued, shaking his head. "That's just wrong. Why would you butcher that word like that? What did it ever do to you?"

"Get out of here. I know what you're doing."

They both did, but it worked. The small smile dancing on her lips was enough for him. He leaned over and kissed the top of her head before going back toward the front door.

"You know I'll be out of touch, but I'll send messages when I can. What's the rule?"

"Never ask details, and remember that if you're contacting, you're all right."

"Good girl. I'll see you soon."

He closed his door behind him, the smile disappearing from his face. The land given to the former Bianchi was on the outskirts of the lands, near the top of the portal city barrier that kept them inside. The high, slightly shimmering magic was just visible on the horizon. It was a message as well as protection—they were not exactly accepted, but they were being given a chance to prove they'd have the pack's back.

He understood it and didn't fault Dominic for the move. It was up to Pasquale's people to make the difference. But they were too scared, too abused under oppressive former leadership, and they no longer had a voice. Nearly half of them hadn't joined with the Lombardi Park, and he couldn't find the wolves who'd left. For all the strength in his nose, they'd alluded him, and it made him edgy. Encantado may have been a massive city with nearly a million or more people packed within it with new influxes, but that didn't mean it was so large they should have been able to disappear from his nose.

Where were his former packmates, and why did he fear what their disappearance would mean for those who remained behind? He wasn't so sure, but he could see the truth in what his sister said in their eyes. The ones who were waiting for him, hovering outside of his home to protect Fabiana … and him. Their Alpha, their nucleus.

For a moment, he let his power unfurl, grow, and swell under his skin. It drank from him as a man parched, exploding into the open space and sending wolves to their knees.

"Protect her while I'm gone."

Pasquale didn't have to shout for his command to reach them. They bowed their heads, but he shook his. He ripped his Alpha call away, locking it deep inside. He was just like his father, demanding when he should ask.

"Please."

Wolves stood to their feet, shaking their heads in confusion.

Fuck, he was no good at this. At ruling. At leading. He didn't know how.

Frustrated, he left.

And those outside watched him lope off. Hope shone in their eyes. He didn't know if he could shoulder it, but he'd try his best.

CHAPTER Six

"Fastest way to cover ground would be to travel through Greenwald Park and directly to Scorched Earth from there."

He was talking, and she should have been listening, but all Giuliana could do was *smell*.

Fresh snow and ... fucking powder. It was feminine. Not a scent she expected to be wrapped around her *mate*. She stepped closer to him, pulling the scent deeper into her lungs. It was familiar, but she couldn't place from where.

Didn't matter though; it wasn't *her* scent.

We can disembowel her. I'm all for that.

For once, she was in complete agreement with her wolf.

"Giuliana."

How fucking dare he! They may not have claimed each other, but they had at least agreed on seeing where things could go. And the bastard thought he could come at her smelling like another woman? He wanted his head between his legs, no longer attached to his freaking neck.

"Giuliana."

She saw fucking red. *RED*.

Mine?

What do you think, sister? He's here smelling like baby ass and you still want to claim him.

Well ... yes. But only after we go wacko on the chick. Then we can make him give all the pleasure we want until we rip his head off too.

We aren't going to kill our mate after we've had fun with him, wolf.

Fine. Have it your way.

"Giuliana!"

"What?"

"Did you hear anything I said?"

She looked at Pasquale. Packed down with deadly weapons and gear for their trip, he was hotter than freaking *life*. The picture was destroyed by the knowledge he'd obviously been around a woman. Giving her a goodbye, maybe.

She'd rip off his damn dick and feed it to him.

"Who is she?"

Pasquale froze, not even breathing as he watched her.

"Cat got your tongue?"

Pussy on his tongue?! Oh, hell no. We don't like cats. Fuck him up, Giuliana!

"Giuliana ..."

Her name was a warning, but she ignored it. He wasn't about to sit here and warn her about shit. Not after what he'd done on her dining room table. Not after he'd given her a choice.

"Who. Is. She?"

Pasquale lifted his head, a muscle working in his jaw. "Fabiana."

That *bitch*. She'd already caused enough of a shit show with Dominic and Zoey. Giuliana thought the woman had learned her lesson, but apparently, she hadn't.

"Gotcha. If you'd excuse me." She stepped to the side to pass him and head out her door, but he moved with her.

"Fabiana isn't your concern."

"She is when the man who's supposed to be mine comes in smelling like her. Now, move."

"I'm not. You won't touch her."

Giuliana growled. "You can't stop me."

"I can, and I will. Fabiana is a member of my former pack. She's important to me. There were other wolves around me too."

But none whose scent permeated his fucking pores.

Important to me.

That's what he'd said. She was *important*. Was she someone he was with before he'd realized he'd found a mate? Fabiana liked Alphas, and she'd always gone after powerful men. She'd played her part so nicely she'd nearly led them to war, and here she was again.

Fuck. Him.

She'd tried. If anyone ever asked, she could have no regrets. She'd attempted to have a normal wolf life, to go with the flow and let things happen. Part of her had looked forward to what it would mean to share a life with another wolf, and she'd ignored the potential bomb of Pasquale releasing his Alpha side in claiming her and what that would mean for her place among the Lombardis.

Coming harder than she ever had before seemed to have addled her brain.

"Fine."

She's important to him.

"Greenwald Park to Scorched Earth, got it. I'll meet you there."

"We're supposed to be on the trail together. You don't have a scenter's nose. He may not be all the way into Scorched Earth, just in that direction."

Giuliana didn't want to admit it, but Pasquale was right. She'd need his nose in order to find Heath and get to the bottom of what was going on. She didn't like it, but she knew she didn't have a choice.

So she'd do what she always did—escape.

Into her head.

Into the mission.

Into the shell.

She wasn't about to deal with this shit and what it meant.

"Lead on, hound. Let's see where my errant packmate has gone."

He lifted a brow at "hound" and glared at her use of "my errant packmate," but she didn't soothe his ruffled feathers. He had *Fabiana* for that. The spineless prick.

Fabiana was everything Giuliana should have been. Soft and delicate, something in need of protecting, and yet sexy and all woman at the same time.

Giuliana couldn't compare.

"Stay downwind of me and follow. A scenter retraces a target's movements until they reach them."

She only nodded, still too angry, too bitter, too fucking hurt to give him any words. He lifted one hand to reach for her, but she jerked away. No, there wouldn't be a repeat performance of earlier. She'd had her blinders ripped off, and the sting would remind her not to fall again.

"She—"

"I don't want to hear it."

"You think I'd—"

"I said I don't."

Pasquale went silent, a mulish expression on his face. *Good for him.* "This isn't over. Keep up."

What the hell is that supposed to mean?

Pasquale was gone, streaking out her front door with mind-blowing speed. She got her wits about her fast enough to follow, stopping long enough to lock her door and clip on her go bag.

Giuliana may not be a scenter, but that didn't mean her wolf's nose wasn't good. She picked up on Pasquale's scent and followed behind him as fast as she could. Traveling from the inner sanctum of their lands to the gates took a dizzying short amount of time, and her lungs labored from the abuse.

She wasn't built to run like a scenter, to track tirelessly in the night. She could maintain her top speed for thirty minutes before she had to slow down, but trailing Pasquale had pushed her beyond that. At his pace, she'd have maybe only half her usual top-speed time.

How the hell is he so quick?

She didn't know, but she was through the gates in record time, sliding out at the exit and heading right. The Greenwald rose in the distance, massive trees just on the other side of the thorny rose bushes that twisted and covered the borders of pack lands. They'd never been able to remove Romano's and Zoey's Miracle Grow magic and now had a second barrier of defense around the walls. Where there had once been a wide expanse of no-man's land between themselves and the Greenwald, there was now only a thin strip of open area about two car lengths wide.

She sucked in a deep breath, rushing oxygen to starving cells as her lungs labored to sustain her and sweat beaded down her forehead. She should have brought the damn car.

She could fool herself into believing she'd left it because exhaust fumes messed with a scenter's nose when they tracked, but she knew she'd done it because Pasquale couldn't stomach being in one. Even when she was fucking pissed at him, she still thought of what would bring him comfort.

If this was what mating did to a wolf, they could count her out of it.

Giuliana wanted to fight him, to get to the bottom of things instead of thinking of him and wondering why. As much as she acted like she did, she didn't actually interact with others on an emotional level very well. Even Zoey and Kalinda looked at her as a babysitter who could make them laugh when the time called for it and protect them when needed.

She'd never had a friend like the way they were together. And she had to admit she was sort of jealous that Silva—a freaking Fae *queen*—had blended in so well, even being new to the group. Giuliana always seemed to be fighting for a place to belong, to be accepted completely for who she was.

It sucked.

She followed Pasquale's scent to the left, heading into the thick of the Greenwald. At least the cool shelter from the trees would help. The darkened interior of the woods was a balm against her heated flesh, sending shivers down her spine. Her eyes adjusted to the change in light as she sniffed to get information from the world around her.

Rabbits to the left. Deer farther downwind, dead center. Life. Her wolf yipped inside, more comfortable here in this space than in the confines of her home. Even with making it as open as she could, there was nothing like the damp darkness of the forest.

Run?

Giuliana reached for her wolf, happy to give up the muddled thoughts of her human side and give fresh lungs a chance to take over. Her wolf sprang forward, wrapping her in love and care so she could sit back for the ride. Yes, she could see through her wolf, smell the hard earth beneath her paws, but she could also sink into her wolf and let her run wild. She held the picture of Pasquale in her head, those intertwining scents, and her wolf followed them.

A branch snapped and her wolf spun, her flexible spine helping her flip in the air and land on her feet facing the threat. A massive white wolf stepped out of nowhere, and she immediately knew the branch was done on purpose. The wolf was too silent, too composed, for such a mistake. Twice her size, and more powerful by far, the wolf lifted its muzzle to the sky and howled.

It was the most beautiful thing she'd ever heard.

A call of the wild.

A cry for being home.

Her throat worked for the chance to join, to lift her head and join the song, but she fought against it.

Pasquale.

Pretty.

If you roll over and open your legs from him, I won't shift for thirty years.

Her wolf sighed, but Giuliana stood her ground. Instead of joining his cry, she balanced her paws wider, lowering her eyes to the side of his head, and snarled.

Unfazed, Pasquale approached her, ears alert and tail high. There was no fear, no hesitation. He was so sure of himself, so controlled.

Hello, pretty girl.

What the fuck? That wasn't her voice or her wolf's that just rang in her head.

Pasquale exposed his teeth. *I know you can hear me.*

Pasquale?

Not exactly.

Her wolf pushed her consciousness aside, brushing past her.

What do you want?

He's hurting.

So is she.

He didn't mean it.

Who is she?

Packmate.

Duh. Try again.

The white wolf shook his head, and Giuliana sat back, wide-eyed. She'd never heard of wolves communicating this way.

Pasquale's wolf sat down on his haunches. *Fabiana is … littermate.*

That explains it. Okay.

Wait. No, that didn't explain shit as far as Giuliana was concerned, no matter *what* her wolf thought. Littermate and packmate were the same thing. How the hell was that an explanation?

Can I mate with you now? I've never seen a wolf so red.

Um, no. And red? She wasn't red. She looked down at her fur. Yeah, it was sort of burgundy under the black, but she wasn't red.

Yes. I've been waiting.

Wrong again! She fought with her wolf as said beast lowered the front of her body to the ground but kept her ass in the air, tail high.

Not happening!

Let him. Mine!

No, you slut. I don't understand.

Giuliana swore her wolf rolled her eyes. *Let the children speak. They don't seem to understand.*

Can I mate you after?

Yes.

No!

Giuliana exploded from her wolf, shifting fast enough to leave her lightheaded and swaying. Strong hands gripped her arms and steadied her.

"Are you okay?"

"Pasquale?"

"Yes. I … apologize for my wolf. He can be pushy."

"Tell me about it."

Pasquale kept his hands on her, his finger tracing circles on her skin.

She liked how that felt.

"I'm going to tell you something no one knows outside my pack because my wolf was at least right about one thing."

"You are *not* mating me right now."

"At least you said right now." She growled in response, and he shook his head with a chuckle. "I get it. Fabiana was the woman you smelled, but it isn't what you think."

"Well, here's your chance to explain it. We don't have time, and we've delayed things long enough. The sooner we get back, the faster we can end all of this."

"She's my sister."

What? "Is … is that what the wolf meant by littermate?"

Pasquale nodded. "For us, the whole pack is family, though we can recognize who we share blood with. The wolf's only way to describe it was to link it to litters."

"He meant that literally. Wait, your sister?"

Pasquale smiled softly. "My younger sister. I was raised to be my father's weapon, not his Alpha. That would mean he'd have to give up power, and he wasn't willing to. Fabiana was easier to control."

Open mouth and insert foot. She really did suck at this, and she'd allowed her fears and self-doubts color her understanding instead of just asking first. Giuliana knew not all Alphas shared a bloodline with previous ones. The strongest wolf would always rule, but in a lot of cases, a child of an Alpha *would* prove to be one as well. It made sense why Pasquale was so strong. But … Fabiana.

Shit. "She's one of those used women, isn't she? That's why you got so upset."

"My father thought her beauty would be useful. Intelligence and power were not. He made sure she knew how to hide very well who she wanted to be."

Well, damn. Now Giuliana felt like shit. The girl was obviously not being taken for who she was, most of the Lombardi Pack hated her, and she'd never be comfortable in a place where she had been intricate in plans of a coup.

"I'm sorry."

Pasquale sighed. "I should have explained better, but I'm used to not claiming her for who she is. It wasn't until my father died that we could even act as siblings. Our people knew, but they were too afraid to go against what my father demanded."

And Giuliana had given in to the prejudice she had against his pack—especially Fabiana. She wasn't naïve to think a simple explanation would smooth things over with many of the pack, but at least she could help it be easier.

"I'll talk to Dominic about her. Zoey's always about the underdog; I know she'd help too."

"We can't."

"Why not?"

"Because when it comes out my father had a son, they will start looking at me as possible challenge to Romano or Dominic.

It's the way of our kind. How long before you think they'd want to push us out?"

He was right, of course. They may walk on two legs, but the wolf inside them would see the power as a challenge, even if the other male wasn't interested in taking position.

"I can see why you said nothing."

"I'm only telling you so you understand something."

"What's that?"

"Claimed or not, you are the only woman I will ever worry about when it comes to being the match for me or my wolf. Claimed or not, you will always have me behind you. This life may have fucked us in having what we wanted, but that doesn't mean I can't be there for you."

Swoon.

Shut up, wolf!

But she was right. Pasquale, for all the weight on his shoulders, was everything Giuliana could have hoped for in a mate. And if this was all they could have, so be it.

CHAPTER SEVEN

Heath's trail overlapped in the Greenwald several times over, slowing them down and spinning them in circles. Pasquale grew frustrated. He trusted his nose and knew it wouldn't steer him wrong. The man *had* been through here. But the skill with which the scent was laid so pristinely worried him.

What if they were off track?

It was possible for a scenter to lose a trail, but it usually was obliterated by water, exhaust, or magic. They hadn't crossed any riverbeds yet, though he could hear them, and obviously no motorized vehicle could travel through the Greenwald. The trees were too densely packed that at times he had to slip through sideways to make it. There were only a few places that allowed for open space on the ground.

And as the sun began to set, he was worried Giuliana may not be able to continue.

She kept quiet, letting him lead, and followed him without complaint, but he wasn't sure she could handle the path like a scenter. For one of them, the scent was all that mattered. Heath's signature was odd, barbed with dark undertones and vegetation Pasquale couldn't quite put his finger on. When he took in the young man's clothes in his room, the scent stayed on the back of Pasquale's tongue in heightened receptors scenters had to use for reserve—much like hounds used the tips of their ears as they dragged them along the ground.

When a scenter caught a scent, he couldn't let it go until he tracked it to where it stopped, like an obsession. Normal wolves needed time to rest.

Still ... the scent aggravated him.

Tracer is going in circles.

Pasquale slid to a stop, his chest heaving as he took in great gulps of air. His wolf was right. There were tracers—scent markers people didn't know they left behind—everywhere. A brush against a tree here, broken branches with minute skin cells attached, the grit of bare feet on ground leaving fading heat. It was the perfect attraction for a scenter. A lure.

"Dammit," Pasquale cursed.

"What is it?"

Pasquale growled, red-hot anger filling his veins. Giuliana stood off to the side, leaning against a tree with her arms folded across her chest. It was a comforting stance, but one he could tell she needed. Her scent was alive with fatigue, her mouth pinched and her nostrils flaring.

Darkness surrounded them, wrapping them in the eerie silence only the night brought. It was ... new, having someone with him while he worked. He wasn't used to explaining things, and even more so uncomfortable because he'd have to tell her he couldn't track him.

He threw back his head and gave in to his nose. The world opened up, brilliant marks of colors and whirls of scent. A normal wolf couldn't do this, see an environment like paint on canvas. The trail of a bunny's flight wound through the trees in a faint blue. A deer's race away from the predators he and Giuliana represented dashed out in frantic purple. The night was vibrant and bright with colors, interlocking stories of their lives, imprints of their existence on earth.

This was what it meant to be a scenter, to see what others could not, to know the world in ways others could never understand. Heath's tracer was a swathe of dark black glittering in the moonlight with threaded silver. It was corded, wrapped, and bundled with spiking green. Pasquale had never seen a scent like that. He reached out and gripped the strands between his fingers.

This was something for him, a gift of his Alpha lineage mixing with his innate scenter calling. His Alpha gift, always hidden, didn't have to be masked with Giuliana. It was freeing, being able to use what was his in the presence of another wolf other than his pack. He'd suppressing it for so long, never giving it a chance to break through the chains he wrapped around it. Now, he let it loose, riding along the trail while he stood still.

His eyes burned, and he knew they glowed with his power. Giuliana sucked in a breath, and he smiled. *This is me, mate. This is who I really am.*

"I need your nose," he called to her.

She stepped forward gingerly. "How can I help?"

"I'm bombarded. Heath's signature is all around me. I need a non-scenter's other senses to help balance it."

"What do I do?"

"Just come here."

When she was within reach, Pasquale used his free hand to pull her in front of him, her back to his front, and wrapped his arms around her, caging her close. He then gripped Heath's tracer in both hands and rested his chin on Giuliana's shoulder.

"Let your wolf reach for mine."

He'd never done this with another wolf besides Fabiana, but he was sure his mate would fit in just well enough.

Wolf, help her bridge.

His wolf snorted. *Feel. She doesn't need help.*

"Oh my gods!"

Is this what you see?

Giuliana's wolf had a smoky, erotic voice that made his wolf shudder inside him. The connection between their human counterparts only made it so the wolves were closer. Pasquale laughed, joy spreading through him. He could see them! Both wolves, his own larger white wolf hovering protectively over Giuliana's reddish-black wolf. They played in the scents, sending sparks up like fireflies in the night, illuminating the darkness with information.

Snake.

Deer.

Mages came this way, but they're gone.

The wolves shot back and forth what they sensed, and Pasquale pulled Giuliana closer, using her gifts to heighten his. She was strong, so strong, of Alpha lineage as well. He didn't know how he hadn't made that connection before.

She was the niece of Arturo Moretti, from a sister long gone—one many didn't speak of—but the same blood ran in her veins. What she didn't have in gifts like him, she had her own. Her wolf lifted its head, searching, reaching.

Giuliana did the same, and it was the most beautiful moment he'd ever experienced in the middle of the forest.

"Blood."

Someone is hurt.

The statements came from her and her wolf at the same time. He remembered Giuliana's gift was for healing. She reached for his hands, the warmth coming from her filled with her power.

"Along this line is blood," she whispered.

"You can see the scent?"

"I see it all."

"Look at me."

When she did, he sucked in a breath. Giuliana was glowing, her eyes as red as the underside of her coat. The color permeated, the same rust hue of what she sensed.

"Show me," he ordered.

Using her to extend his control, he yanked on the scent to straighten it so it would lead them where they had to go.

"Run with me but stay connected."

Giuliana only nodded as they sprang forth, humans and wolves, keeping sight on the tracer they followed. She moved with the same determination as a scenter, tirelessly, giving herself over to the hunt.

She's a healer, and she's as driven as you to do what she's meant for.

He agreed with his wolf, following her stead and keeping them on track. Each step was silent. They were predators, meant to stalk this sort of terrain and pick apart their prey. Never, in all his years, had he heard of a connection quite like this.

Even when he'd worked with Fabiana, she hadn't been able to see the scents. She only became more aware of them. He'd done it when she asked about how he viewed the world, the studier in her intrigued. But this … this was something else entirely.

They were working together instead of him directing the way. Now that Giuliana had sensed the blood in a way only she could, he was able to as well. It wasn't a scent as much as it was a feeling in the pit of his stomach, a gnawing in his gut he had to fix.

The Greenwald sped past, the trees a murky backdrop to a night alive with power. They zipped through the trees, never stopping, heading straight toward the end.

They came to a small clearing, soft grass swaying in the delicate breeze. It should have been beautiful, this place where the moonlight touched the earth. It should have been a space to camp out for the night before they moved on.

Instead, it was slick with the eerie black of blood in the night. Each blade of grass was splattered with it.

Heath.

Wolves.

My wolves!

Pasquale staggered to a stop beside Giuliana and surveyed the scene before him. What the hell was going on? He shouldn't smell his pack in this scent of destruction. They never should have been here.

But all the blood was Heath's.

All the signs pointed to a vicious wolf attack.

There were paw prints pressed into sticky congealing blood, perfectly preserved. Blood-caked fur was trapped under the paw prints.

Pasquale used his nose, but Giuliana bent next to the grass and put her hands out, palms down. "There's enough blood that whoever was attacked should be dead."

Not who … Heath. The both knew it. She was tied enough to his ability that she knew exactly whose blood was here.

"Giuliana—"

She shook her head, cutting him off. "He can't be dead. You smelled him heading to Scorched Earth."

"We're in the direction of it, Giuliana."

She balled her fists. "And what wolves did this? I'd recognize our pack immediately, and even the Moonstone to the south. My uncle dealt with them a lot when we built the Arena, as they are over the entertainment sector. These weren't their wolves."

No, they weren't. And he didn't want to tell her. Didn't want his people to face any more bullshit. But when she turned teary eyes to him, he couldn't lie to her. Couldn't destroy what little bond they had.

Who was he kidding? This would ruin *everything*.

He lifted his head, squaring his shoulders. For a moment, he just looked at her. Beautiful, even now, with pain etched over her features and rage in her gaze. The gentle slope of her neck, the way she crouched, ready to spring, and her lush curves on display. This wasn't how he wanted to remember her, but he memorized it anyway.

Before hate filled her.

Before the dream of what could have been turned into a nightmare.

Life was a bitch—one that had ruined them long before they laid eyes on each other.

And in the last couple of days, they'd already gone through a tremulous level of back and forth.

No, mating was never in their cards.

"Bianchi wolves."

She froze. "There are no Bianchi wolves anymore."

"Our pack once boasted just over a hundred packmates. With the failed coup, we lost a third of that number, and then half more when some did not choose to join the Lombardis."

Giuliana stood slowly, stretching to her full height, her canines bursting in her mouth. This was the Enforcer of the Lombardi Pack, not the woman he'd given pleasure to, not the partner he'd hunted with.

"I want to make things very clear right now. Are you saying your former packmates who didn't stay with us *attacked* one of ours? Are you saying the text message Lorenzo received may have been a plant?"

That connection was a good one to make, and one made with lightning speed. "Primo taught subterfuge with an iron fist. Ottavio just gave him the opportunity he needed to use it against Arturo."

And there it was.

The reminder.

History.

Ottavio, cousin to Arturo, had been part of his pack and planned to kill him with Primo's help. They'd failed, but the rippling effect of the move still rocked the foundations. An intricate span of players—Ottavio of the Moretti Pack; Primo and Luigi, Alpha and *Capo* of the Bianchi; and Benedict of the Mage Council—had destroyed so many lives. Their deaths didn't make up for what they'd made others lose.

"Fucking dogs."

Her words cut. They were his people, even if he could see what this meant. The difference between them was, he could step back and wonder *why*. Giuliana just saw betrayal, and fuck if he couldn't understand.

"They are leaderless. We don't know what Heath may have done."

"Dominic will want blood. *I* want blood."

Pasquale nodded. "I understand."

What else was he supposed to say? What could he do? At this moment, with Alpha power or not, he was a lower-ranking wolf in the structure and his Enforcer had just spoken.

Giuliana hesitated. Reaching out to him, she let her hand fall back to her side. "He's my Alpha, Pasquale."

I should be.

A toss-away thought, but once realized, he couldn't help the rage boiling inside him. *He* should be her Alpha. *He* should be the one she gave allegiance to.

He should be the only man whose needs she'd fight to meet.

But it wasn't like that and thinking like a Neanderthal wouldn't help the situation. The fact remained that some of *his* people had attacked one of hers. There would be no leaping across that fucking divide. Dominic had a right to want those responsible to pay. And Pasquale couldn't shake the feeling the perpetrators had purposefully hidden the trail to throw him off.

That sense of betrayal ran deep.

They knew he'd be the one to follow, as there was no one better than him, and they'd done it anyway.

We're animals, Pasquale.

Maybe his father had been right all along. He and Fabiana were chasing a fucking dream, trying to pick up the pieces of what remained.

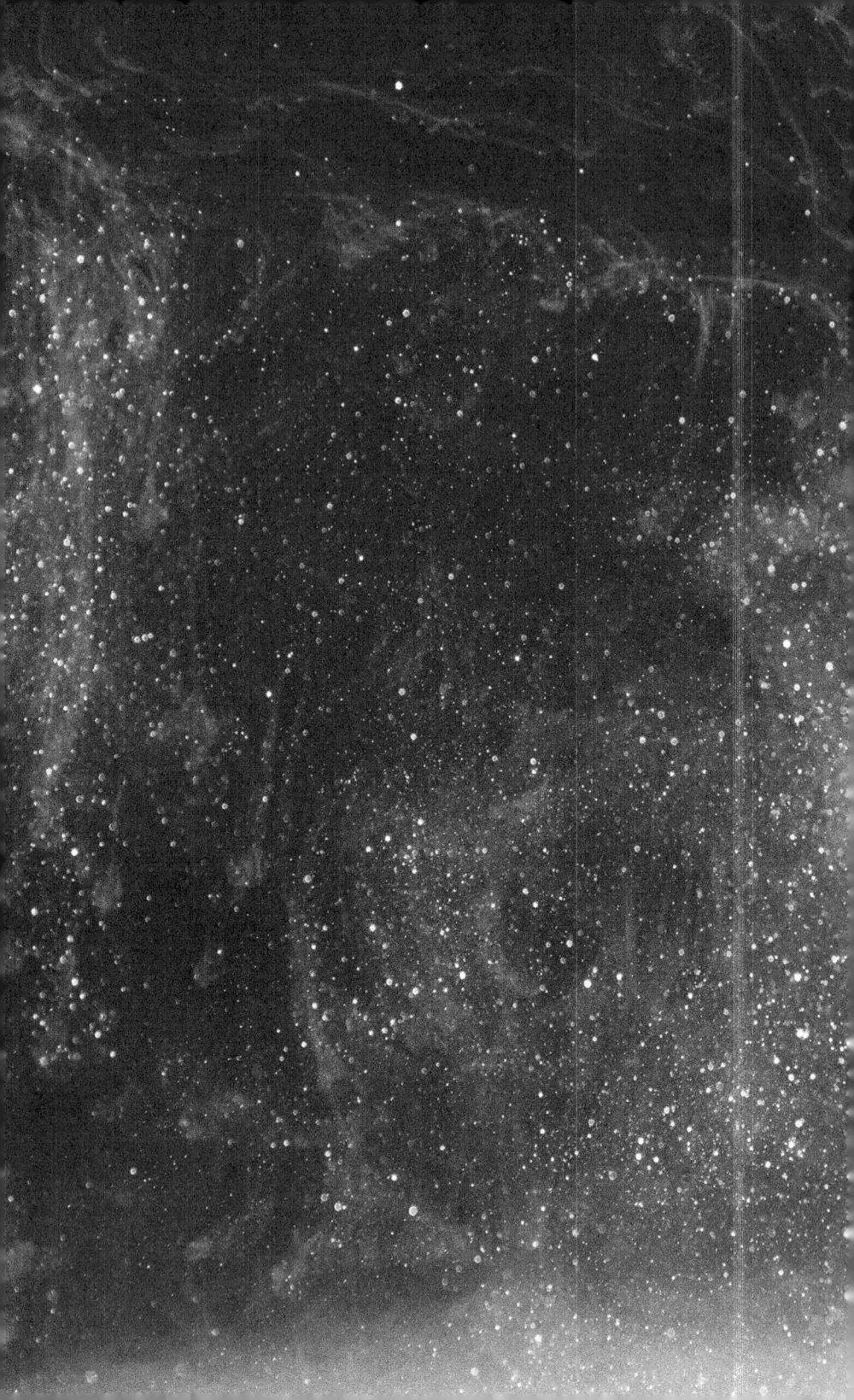

CHAPTER *Eight*

"I want all the Bianchi members rounded up."

Well, of course he did. Dominic stalked back and forth in his living room, rage radiating in waves. Zoey, stomach growing so much larger, sat with her feet curled up under her and rubbed her belly as she watched her mate with worried eyes. Giuliana detected pain off the Alpha mate and wondered what complication she was having. Dominic hadn't said much of anything.

"Dominic—"

"Not now, Zoey."

"Don't you yell at me, you overgrown gorilla."

Giuliana blinked, swallowing the urge to burst out laughing. Dominic whirled on his mate. "I am *not* a damn monkey."

"I didn't call you a monkey."

He scoffed. "You just called me a gorilla!"

"Yeah, not monkeys."

Dominic stared at his mate incredulously. "Zoey, maybe you need to lie down."

"They're apes, Dom. *Apes.*" She shook her head.

"Zoey," he growled in warning.

Not afraid at all, Zoey pointed at her mate. "You can't make a whole pack responsible for a few bad apples, and we don't know what happened."

"She's right, Alpha. We only know their scent was there."

This response only made Dominic glare at Giuliana. She was *really* tired of the glaring thing he'd been doing since she and Pasquale had returned. They'd waited two days to do anything, as Dominic had been livid and deadly. Thank gods for Zoey keeping him busy with crazy demands to get ready for the baby.

The reprieve could only last so long.

Pasquale stood beside Giuliana, feet spread shoulder-width apart and hands clasped behind his back. He'd been quiet the whole time, keeping his head down so he wasn't viewed as a challenge for Dominic, but now his gaze was riveted to the Alpha.

Rounding up his pack would be a fucking death sentence for them, and they all knew it. It was a struggle for Giuliana not to reach out and soothe him. But she couldn't—not then. Dominic would notice the move, and it would start another line of questioning she wasn't ready to deal with.

But … what could she do? This was her pack. He may be her mate, but they weren't mated yet, so she had no claim. Still, she was torn in two. Revenge for her people, or console her mate?

This was a mess.

Her wolf was going fucking bananas, out for blood for Heath and wanting to protect Pasquale at the same time. It made her skin itchy, pulling things taut.

Mine.

He is, but Dominic is our Alpha.

Snort. *For now.*

Don't start, wolf.

But he's hurting, and Snow is ready to break.

Snow?

An impression of Pasquale's large white wolf filled Giuliana's mind. *You named his wolf?*

Why not? You all have names. I'm Red. Hot, right?

Giuliana rolled her eyes. *Okay. Focus.*

If I focus, I'll want to fight again.

Point taken.

"Fine. Tell me what you saw, Giuliana."

Dominic didn't acknowledge Pasquale, and Giuliana wasn't about to have that. She may understand his rage, but Pasquale hadn't been the wolf responsible.

"Pasquale was able to track the scent to the far reaches of the Greenwald, where he found the clearing. Blood covered the ground, and with my knowledge, I assumed there was enough to kill a person. It doesn't mean he's dead, but if he's alive, I don't know how he would've gotten away."

"Was there a trail out?"

"No, Alpha. Only trail leading away was that of the wolves."

"The *Bianchi* wolves."

Giuliana gritted her teeth. "Yes, Alpha."

Finally, Dominic's gaze swung to Pasquale. "Which wolves?"

Pasquale didn't falter, and Giuliana couldn't help a sense of pride swelling in her chest. Her mate was not weak, he wasn't afraid. He'd stand up for what he believed in.

Head thrown back, Pasquale answered. "The wolves who didn't join with the Lombardis."

Romano, always there, always by Dominic's side, shifted from his stance in the corner of the room. Kalinda had been buried at the Trinity Council offices with Silva the last few days, and it freed Romano to be on hand for anything.

The large wolf rolled his shoulders, the grips of his holstered handgun catching the light for a moment. "How do you know?"

"By smell."

"Garbage must be killer for you," Romano retorted. His normal joking mannerism leaked through, but the edge to his voice stripped it of levity.

"Most times it burns my ass hairs."

Romano blinked at Pasquale's response before chuckling. "Good one."

"Dominic, you know not all of my former pack came over with the blend. There were some who relished how Primo ruled, the dark power he infused in them. They saw the way things were going and—" Pasquale stopped and glanced over at Zoey.

"What?" Giuliana growled at Dominic's harsh tone.

She swallowed the sound when he frowned at her. *Shit.* That wasn't really keeping things cool. Pasquale took one step over, slightly in front of her, taking Dominic's attention.

Well, this isn't subtle at all.

But it worked.

"He had a group of men who were his Enforcers. They were the cruelest. Not meant to be *Capos*, but soldiers to do his bidding. The Renegades."

The Renegades. She remembered that name from somewhere but couldn't remember why. It was on the tip of her tongue, but no matter how much she tried, she couldn't grasp it.

The Renegades are coming, little one. Hide. Hide away.

Giuliana shook her head. What the hell was that? The … voice. So smooth, so deep, but feminine. Her wolf whimpered but gave no answer.

"The Renegades are a myth. A thing of the past. They were wreaking havoc in Boulder, but in the early years before portal cities were even planned. In a time when wolves weren't contained like they are now. And Primo was not their leader," Dominic argued.

Pasquale shook his head. "Primo always wanted to rule Encantado. In his mind, the main families should have been Bianchi and DeLuna."

"The DeLunas are the Moonstone Pack's leading family. They run the entertainment district."

"So you're saying they are weak? Maybe Primo thought he could rule them," Zoey mused.

Dominic snorted. "There's a reason the Moonstone Pack acts as liaison between the mages and wolves. They could kick our asses if they wanted to."

Zoey's draw dropped. "What?"

Romano shrugged. "As much as I hate to admit it, and I'd never say it in front of one of the bastards, but they are the largest singular pack in Encantado. With the Morettis allied with the Lombardis, it makes us comparable, but we're under two Alphas while they are under one. Their sheer size gives them the big dick on campus."

"And their control over the southern side of Encantado is absolute. We've tipped the balance with Kalinda and Silva on our side, but going against them would mean war. Too many would die," Dominic explained.

Pasquale reached back and touched Giuliana, his fingertips barely grazing the top of her hand. She liked that small caress. She shifted closer to him, sinking into his heat.

I'm here.

He took a steadying breath. "Primo knew he couldn't beat them, but if he was measurable in size, absorbing Moretti's pack would have made them equal. At least then they'd have to have a truce directed by the Council."

"And he would have had an in with Benedict," Zoey surmised.

"Exactly. And with the Renegades by his side, he would have eventually picked at the Moonstone's numbers with Council help."

Romano shook his head. "Primo had it all planned out, the bastard. Didn't work out that way in the end."

Dominic rubbed his chin. "Okay, say I believe you, and Primo had the Renegades. Why would they attack Heath?"

Hide! Don't come out until I come for you. Promise me, Lana. Promise me.

Giuliana groaned, grabbing her head. Pasquale turned quickly, taking her into his arms. "What is it?"

But she couldn't speak, couldn't acknowledge him. Words and pictures morphed in her head too fast for her to grasp and understand. Hands pushing her into a closet, the inky black of the space closing around her, snarls and snapping teeth echoing in her ears.

Breathe, Giuliana.
I can't.
It'll pass.
What is this, Red?
Memories.
I don't know what is going on.
Breathe.
I am fucking breathing.
Hide!

The scream ripped through her skull, ricocheting inside and cracking as it went. Giuliana grabbed her head. Dominic, Romano, and Pasquale may have hollered, Zoey screamed for her, but Giuliana was trapped. She couldn't fight, couldn't get away.

Breathe.
I'm scared, Red.
You were then too. But I'm here, just like before.

Her wolf didn't sound like she always did, sarcastic and biting. Now she was soothing, a balm to frayed nerves. She almost sounded … motherly.

Red.

You were never alone, Giuliana. I've always been what you need, when you need it. Let me take it.

Red …

Let go, Giuliana. I'm here.

She sank, fading into the darkness. Warm fur wrapped around her, heat and power. Her claws exploded from her fingers.

Let go.

Don't hurt anyone, okay?

Never. You will see.

"Shif—"

"Don't make her."

Dominic's Alpha call wrapped around her, freezing her shift mid-motion. Her cells burned, screeching to a standstill instantly, but Pasquale's demand broke the power. She rushed for her change, pulling it around her.

"Are you out of your fucking mind? She's going feral and my wife is here. Shif—"

"She won't, and she is my *mate*."

The world froze. Romano in front of Zoey, crouched low and teeth bared. Dominic was in front of Pasquale, his gaze riveted on Giuliana but the warning in position clear. He'd rip Pasqual apart to get to her. But Pasquale didn't move or back away.

He stood firm, his hand out to her the whole time.

Red?

Snow!

Safe?

She's scared. She can't be scared, not like this.

We will protect her.

Giuliana landed on all fours in the room, muzzle up in the air and sitting on her haunches. The memories weren't so loud now. They faded to a buzz on the edge—insistent, but not clear enough to hurt anymore.

Good. He smells good.

Warm fingers threaded through the thick scruff right behind her ear, and her tongue lolled out of her mouth. She like that, a lot. Pressing her body into the touch, she whined softly.

"What the fuck is wrong with you?" Dominic raged.

Male, don't piss me off.
He's our Alpha.
Red snorted. *Alpha or not, he won't be much if I bite off his balls. What happened?*
This voice was Pasquale's instead of Snow, and Red liked the way he sounded too. A lot.
The past.
What?
She almost remembered what she can't remember.
Something with the Rene—
Don't say that name. She is hanging on by a thread right now.
Is it easier not to ask about that, Red?
For now, yes. She's never been able to face it.

He was talking to her wolf, and she heard the conversation but it didn't register. None of it did, really. They were words on a page in a language she was barely aware of. They slid into blankness as soon as they stopped talking. And that was fine with Giuliana. She didn't want to think.

It was much easier to just be. To enjoy this moment. The snow and fresh dirt scent wafting off her mate. His heat suffusing her skin and warming her. The way he protected her. She liked that much better.

"She needs this," Pasquale said out loud.

Hmmm, she agreed. Needed him.

"Are you talking to her? Is that what can happen between wolf-to-wolf mating?"

Zoey's voice was tinkling bells. That was awesome. Giuliana didn't realize how much she liked that sound. She stood to her feet, wanting to get closer to it.

Pretty.
You can't approach the Alpha mate like this.
But I want to meet the female.
You know Zoey, Red.
No … not her. The other *female. Alpha.*

Pasquale clenched her neck, holding her in place. *That's sort of hot.*

"Dominic, uh …"
"What?"
"She wants to meet the Alpha female."

All this talking was really irritating her. She was driven, pulled to put her nose to Zoey's stomach, and the stupid males were stopping her.

"Giuliana."

Giuliana lifted her head at Dominic's call. Or at least she thought she did, but her wolf only had eyes for Zoey.

"Red."

That's me.

Her wolf lifted her head and looked at Pasquale and huffed.

"Who the fuck is Red?" Romano stood to his full height, the immediate threat gone.

"Her wolf. Look, it's a lot to explain. But Giuliana or her wolf would never hurt Zoey. You know this. Talking about the … myth upset her."

"The myth?" After a moment, Dominic's face cleared. "Fuck."

"Do you know why?"

"Back off. You haven't claimed her yet, and she's still my Enforcer. I don't have to tell you shit. That's her choice. Giuliana … or Red. Go see Zoey."

Finally.

Pasquale let her go, and she hesitated for a moment. She really liked his hands on her, but she had to get to the Alpha female. Decisions, decisions. After a moment, Pasquale placed his hand on her neck again.

"Let's go."

She moved with him, heading right to Zoey. The small woman with the rounded belly sat back in her chair and blinked. "You have really big teeth, Giuliana."

Scared. You scare her.

I'll be gentle.

Giuliana lowered her tail and ears, whimpering as she pressed herself to the floor. She crawled, scooting across the floor until she rested at Zoey's feet.

"Thank you. Now, I'm really sort of scared shitless of you biting my belly, so if you could sort of not do that, I'd love that."

Giuliana and Red both snorted at that but lifted their head as gently as possible, pressing their nose to her stomach. A wave of power rippled through the room as Zoey's stomach moved.

"She's moving!"

The baby pressed back against Giuliana's nose. Her Alpha call was different than the males. More subtle, searching, but no less powerful. It slipped around Giuliana, pulling her in before she realized she was ensnared.

"I don't think you have to worry about the baby letting anyone hurt her momma if they are shifter."

Pasquale's words made Giuliana go *duh* in her head, but men were slow and sometimes needed some help with simple understanding.

She's strong, like you.
Awe, thanks Red. But I'm not a female Alpha.
No, but you'll help shape her.
Thank you.
For what?
I feel better now.
Always.
You know I love Snape, right?
Who doesn't? He was the bravest man we knew.
You just quoted the last line! Ugh, you're the best wolf ever. You know that?
Love you too, Giuliana.
I won't threaten to not shift for thirty years again.
Can I mate with Snow now?
I take back my last statement.
Knew it.

But she did feel better. The Alpha female moved away from her, and the power receded in the room. Giuliana could breathe, finally, without thinking her brain was going to explode. She'd have to deal with explaining, maybe, but for now it seemed everyone in the room was just giving her what she needed.

Family.

This was what family did, and she couldn't help acknowledging the fact Pasquale was still at her side, in the center of it all.

"You can shift back now?"

She nodded and reached for her change. She was standing at Pasquale's side when it finished, her head not as clouded as before.

"We won't round up the Bianchi, but you're taking point on finding the men who hurt Heath. Romano, reach out to Boulder and see if there's been anything going on, or if they have information on the group that shall not be named so Giuliana doesn't lose her shit again."

Snort. They're Voldemort.

She bit her lip not to laugh at her wolf. Yeah, she got the reference, and laughing about it would be easier than falling back down the crazy path.

"Will do. They may have more insight on their movements and patterns. Anything to help us figure out why and where they could be."

"Pasquale, you will bring the Bianchi wolves more into the fold. We need any information we can get on these guys, and we also will need some of your best men together to hunt them. We can't do this with just you and Giuliana. After we've gathered what we can, we plan our next move."

She let out a pent breath. At least he wasn't condemning an entire pack based on what a few had done, for now, and they had some heading on what was going on.

But …

"Who's going to talk to Lorenzo?"

And that would be the worst moment of all. How do you tell someone their best friend was gone? Zoey hit the nail right on the head.

"I will," Giuliana offered. "You can't take that sort of emotion right now. I'll take care of it."

"Do you want me to go with you?"

Pasquale, the man meant to be her mate, was right there taking the step beside her. Showing her what it could be. But the divide would grow. What the Bianchis had done, been involved with, grew more and more horrible with each passing action. Eventually, Dominic wouldn't be able to stomach them if this kept going.

And what would that mean for them?

When he realized Pasquale was Primo's son. When Zoey knew Fabiana was his sister. When they realized Giuliana knew all of this and hadn't told them.

She didn't know if she could think of it, or how it would all turn out. So she only focused on the fact he stood beside her now, that he'd follow her wherever this would lead.

"Yeah, I'd like that."
Because there was no telling when he'd be gone.

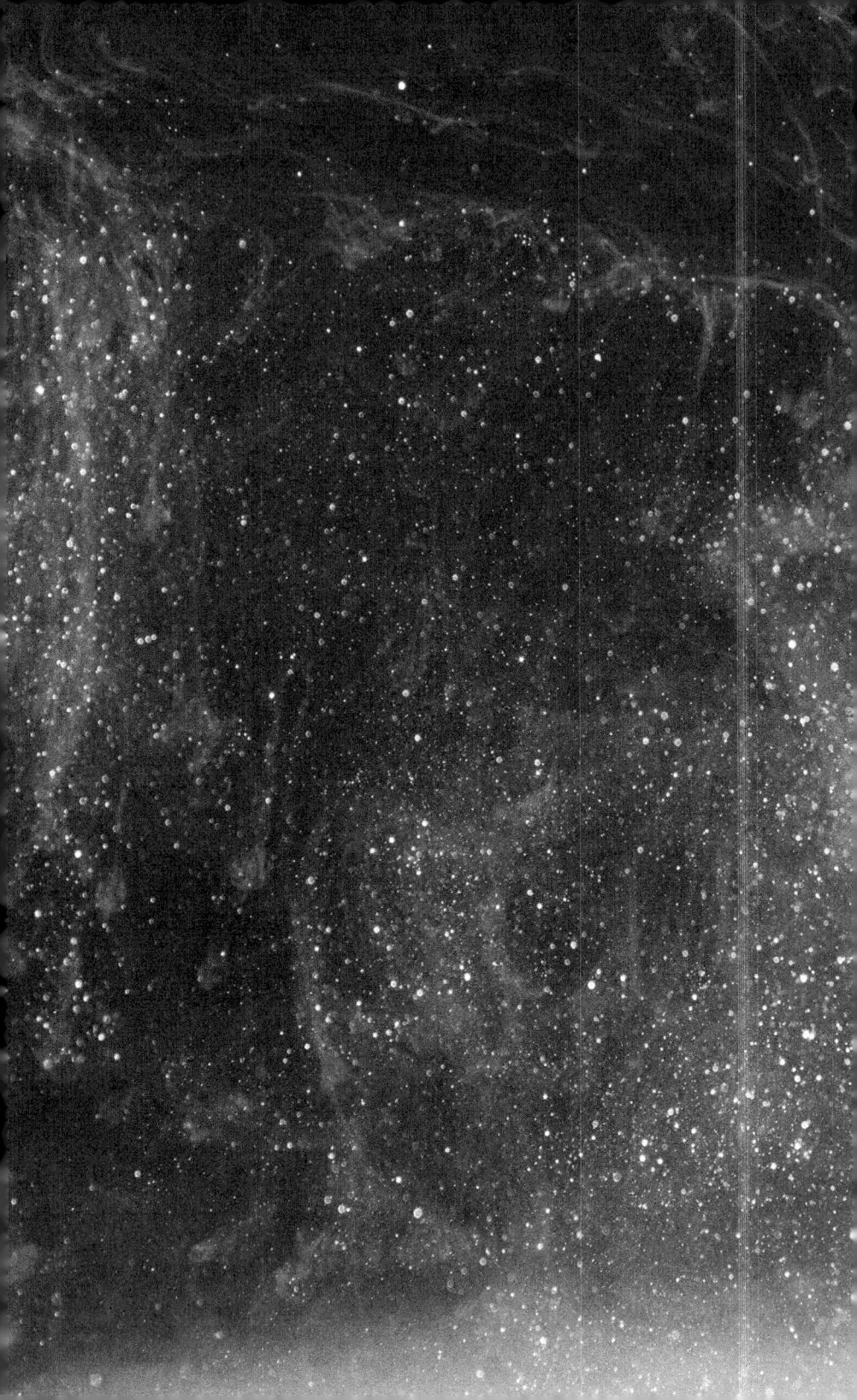

CHAPTER Nine

Kalinda rubbed the back of her aching neck and sighed. Okay, so being the head bitch in charge of the Trinity Council was amazing and all that jazz, but she really wished she could just have a break. The National Council was making much ado about nothing—aforementioned "nothing" being her position as Ales.

Turns out it was much rarer than Silva, her *Cosantiór*, had told them.

Like … to the tune of there were *none*.

Well, except for Kalinda, and that meant Kalinda's Katering was predominately handled by her handpicked baker with Kalinda only able to complete orders once a month. Of course, it led to big bank when people knew she was the one actually making their order instead of infusing it with her power through the baker.

Big bucks notwithstanding, Kalinda was freaking *tired*. And her pack—that was something she was getting used to saying—was hurting, with one of their own missing. She hadn't gotten many updates from Romano about it.

It was something they agreed on, keeping their work as separate as possible. It was enough she was the leader of the Trinity, and it gave the Lombardi Pack a hefty lift in social standing and power. But internally, she never made a move for them to keep things neat and tidy, so she didn't have mages out searching Encantado for Heath even when she *really* wanted to.

"You're doing that frowny thing that makes your forehead look like a sideways vagina."

Kalinda flicked her hand, sending a heavy paperweight right at her *Cosantiór's* lovely face. Silva ducked and let it slam into the wall, sending plaster and wood everywhere.

"If that had hit me, it would have smashed my face!" Silva yelled.

Kalinda blew her a kiss. "A marked improvement."

Silva snorted. "At least your sense of humor is still intact."

That was something Kalinda had to put squarely on the shoulders of her mate. Just thinking of him made her hot. He'd taught her how to let go, to laugh, to give into her emotions. The iron will she had allowed her to control her skill better with each passing day, but the level of freedom she had in being herself made her magic all the stronger.

Slay.

Silva perched on the couch in Kalinda's office—the former solarium of the Mage Council's headquarters. The place had a major remodeling after she took office, pushing Amalia, Lennox, and Yon into the west wing of the estate so she had the entire east wing to deal with her business. Not that she stayed there often, because home was where Romano was, but she had times where she had to spend days on site, and it had enough space to house Silva and her collection.

The Fae Queen had slowly started gathering items from her homeland that showed up in portal cities from across the country. Spent a pretty penny too, but there was nowhere safer for it to be. Silva still couldn't get back home just yet, and she wasn't so sure she wanted to. According to her, leaving Kalinda unprotected wasn't an option, and Kalinda wasn't ready to travel through the Chaos Realm to get there.

Yeah, that was a well-kept secret Kalinda hadn't been able to share with her pack or mate. The Chaos Realm was actually a byway from the Fae world to the Human one, a separation only those who had Fae blood could traverse without losing their goddamn minds. But for some reason, the Chaos Realm wasn't letting Silva near it without sending her magic into a dangerous spiral.

Silva snapped her iridescent wings—today's color was cherry-red to match her dress—and rested them over the back of the seat. "Where are the Three Stooges?"

"My *Trinity* are currently on assignment to the FBMC to get me further literature on the Pendulum Swing of the 1950s."

"So … busy work."

"Partially. As much as I want to hate them for trying to wreck my life, Lennox did believe the Ales was to be controlled by the Trinity, based on the little information he was afforded from the National level. Can't *really* blame them for what they attempted."

"What about what they did to Zahara?"

"That's why I said partially. Benedict had a lot more to do with it, but they shouldn't have let him run wild like that. Maybe if they hadn't, Dominic would have grown to know his mother and had a different life."

"Not that I want to get philosophical, but there are reasons for everything. If he hadn't lost her the way he did, he may never have met Zoey, or you wouldn't have met Romano."

There was that. She couldn't argue what they'd done had indeed given a new path to the ones they'd tried to control. But Kalinda still couldn't look them in the face without wanting to punch them, so she sent them away.

"Either way, understanding how the Pendulum Swing occurred may help us ensure it doesn't happen again."

The Pendulum Swing of the 1950s had spewed magic into the Human world from the Fae—an amount no one was prepared for. It forced those with magical gifts to be exposed and their number increased. Of course, there was magic long before that moment. Kalinda's bloodline was a testament to that fact, but their public awareness wasn't something they'd had to contend with. And since the Chaos Realm was still very dangerous, and twisted beyond what it once had been, Kalinda wanted to understand why.

Why were there no more of the Ales bloodlines?

Why was the concentration of magic so diluted to where only a few held great power?

In essence, the lower mage plight was a microcosm of other issues in the world, and Kalinda was going to do what she could.

"When are they set to come back?"

Kalinda stretched in her seat, joints popping as they realigned. "When they have something useful."

"That could be *forever*."

"That's fine with me."

"You're such a bitch, and I love you for it."

"Of course, you do."

They laughed, a moment of levity in the otherwise fast-paced job Kalinda had taken on. It's why she appreciated having Silva with her. The Fae wasn't just a pretty face; she could be a drill sergeant when needed, and she also made sure Kalinda was never bored. And while she didn't remember everything from her past, she was slowly regaining some of the regal thought processes Kalinda relied on when she was working with Encantado policy.

Kalinda, a politician. Who would have thunk it?

Silva's laughter cut off abruptly and she twisted around to face the door into the office.

"What is it?"

"Lennox."

"What? They only left a week ago. They shouldn't be back so soon."

The powerful Level 9 mage walked into her office without a knock, though he bowed at her. "Good afternoon, Ales."

Kalinda frowned at him. "I have a door for a reason."

"Yeah, for knocking. Or fucking against."

Kalinda barely refrained from sputtering at Silva's addition. Not that she was wrong, but … "Did you find something?"

Lennox's white hair glowed in the sun streaming in from outside, appearing almost to flicker. It was a testament to his greatest affinity to fire. Long, slender fingers danced with sparks of flame as he stepped closer.

"In a manner of speaking."

Silva jumped to her feet. "Shields up."

But the call came a bit too late, and a force slammed into Kalinda, tossing her away from her desk and shooting pieces of paper into the air. In slow motion, the pieces fluttered in the wind, and Silva expanded her wings. Lennox's smile was deadly, and his gaze was focused on Kalinda.

"It's time for things to change, Ales. You'll excuse me if I'm a bit rough. I'm a little rusty."

What the hell is he talking about?

There was no time. Lennox threw his hands in the air, palms facing outward, and whispered an incantation. Silva used her wings to push into the air, spinning in a circle to slam into him, but he didn't budge. Silva was blasted away, careening into the wall with a sickening *thud*.

"Silva!"

"Ah, ah, ah. I think all eyes should be on me."

The fear in Silva's gaze as she looked at Kalinda made Kalinda's blood run cold. Silva was pale, her violet eyes sparking with power but dancing with abject terror. No one should have been able to do that to her.

Silva forced herself to her feet again and lashed, her body a blur. Lennox dodged, slipping like water and striking out with claws. Sprinkles of blood splattered to the floor. Swinging wide, Silva used her leg to sweep at Lennox's feet, but he leapt, twisting mid-air. Landing on her leg as if he weighed nothing, he punched her.

They went back and forth, trading blows at rapid speed until Lennox pressed one palm out in front of him. "*Wynathraeda.*"

Kalinda didn't understand the word Lennox spoke, but it was decidedly *not* English, and not in a tone of voice she'd ever heard him use. And it sent Silva spinning back to the ground.

Silva coughed, struggling to get to her knees. "*Welhuroth ren uthu?*"

Lennox looked over at her, the wind picking up out of nowhere and spinning around him. Kalinda and Silva were pinned by the force. Kalinda groaned under the weight, her ribs pressed hard against the marble floor. She reached inside for her Ales gift, pulling from those spirits she carried deep in her heart.

But they were silent.

Nothing.

Just darkness.

Come to me!

No response.

"Here's a better question, *Quinuneestanay*. Who are *we*?"

Lightning exploded, the sound loud enough to make Kalinda scream and her ears ring. She curled into herself, unable to grasp her magic as a large, gaping maw of black opened against the wall next to Silva. Four men stepped through in gleaming armor of black and red.

If she could call them men.

They were tall, so fucking tall, with impossibly broad shoulders and sharp fangs hanging over their bottom lips. *Daywalkers?* Kalinda knew there were vampires in Encantado, but she'd never dealt with them. Most chose to live in outskirt portal cities. But as she continued to look at them, she reevaluated. They had pointed ears and eyes dark as night.

"Unseelie!" Silva screeched.

Kalinda couldn't make sense of a thing, didn't know what to do.

Something in Silva changed. Her face grew red, thin blue veins spreading like a spiderweb across her skin, and she lifted to her feet without touching a thing.

"You are not welcome here."

"Like we've ever followed *your* rules."

What the fuck was going on? Lennox was not Fae. Silva would have been aware of that, right? This didn't make sense.

"Allow me to formally introduce myself. I am Kieran of the Shadow."

The visage of Lennox faded and morphed. He grew taller, his shoulders broader and stronger. His face turned pale, nearly white, with dark eyes full of silvery stars, a short beard curling over his jaw. Long black hair whipped around his face in the maelstrom, but he seemed unaffected.

He was painfully beautiful, nearly impossible to look at, and he sported the same sharp teeth and pointed ears as his companions.

The men in armor surrounded Silva, pointing wicked spears at her neck. A howl cutting through the air chilled Kalinda to the bone. It was a call to war, to blood and bones, nothing like what she'd heard from the Lombardi Pack.

Five large wolves, all black, leapt through the maw Kieran had created and surrounded him.

"You see, you should have stayed hidden, *Niamh Danaan of the Silver.*"

Silva spat at him, uncaring of the spears ready to tear her apart.

Kalinda struggled to reach out a hand. "Don't. Silva."

Violet eyes met Kalinda, and the pain there popped like rubber against the skin. "I have to save you."

Kalinda tried to shake her head, but she couldn't move anymore. The wind grew more forceful, forcing her face against the ground and sending electric shocks of pain across her cheekbone.

"I claim *hilosnaril*."

The word made the room grow too bright as it filled with golden sparks and vibrating power. The Fae near Silva lowered their spears a bit.

Kieran cocked his head to one side. "The Seelie have no honor to claim such."

Silva looked at Kalinda. "I will give my blood to bind it."

Kieran stalked toward her, the wolves keeping pace with him. Kalinda knew, without a doubt, the only reason Silva didn't fight with everything she had was because there was greater risk of Kalinda being harmed than she could stomach.

The realization made Kalinda sick. The bond between the two of them was a double-edged sword. It may have made Kalinda stronger, but it weakened the Fae Queen.

Always bound to her.

Always to follow.

When Kieran reached Silva, he pressed one nail to her throat and punctured her skin with a slow, deliberate push. Silva gritted her teeth but didn't cry out. As the blood trickled down his nail, it snaked around his finger before soaking into his flesh.

"Accepted. And in case someone else decides to come to the party …" In a flash, Kieran was at Kalinda's side.

"No!"

Silva's scream echoed as fire burned its way over Kalinda's legs.

Romano …

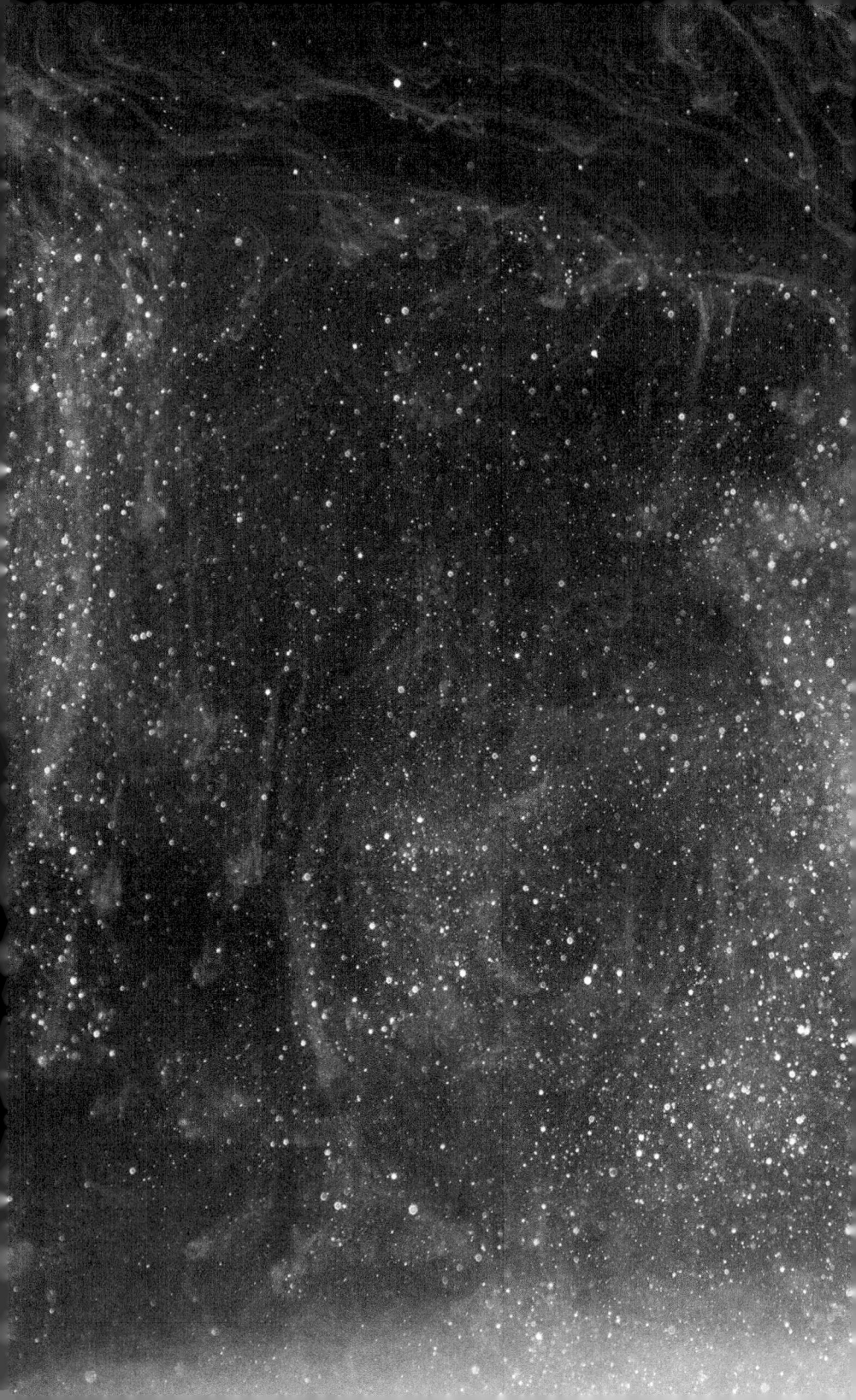

CHAPTER TEN

Lorenzo was nothing more than a kid, really. He'd grown up with the Lombardi Pack, and he and Cin were taking the world by storm. With his fiancée's jewelry and his computer sense, there was nowhere to go but up. The couple had recently moved in together and out of the Community Center apartments Dominic had made in honor of the teens.

If he kept going the way he was going, he'd be Made in no time, despite his mother's apprehension.

But today … Giuliana wanted to be anywhere else other than at his door. She'd worn her armor, black pants and tank top with her shit kicker boots. Her hair was pulled back in a bun at the nape of her neck, and her weapons were strapped to her. She looked as deadly as she was.

Romano and Dominic favored priceless suits, decadence to hide their savagery, and most days Giuliana wore the top name brands to match them. It didn't seem right to come to Lorenzo like that.

The only accessory she'd brought was Pasquale, and his quiet presence at her shoulder buoyed her. He was close enough his heat slipped over her skin, but not so much he made her claustrophobic.

"How well did he know Heath?"

"Not long, but it's *how* he knew him. Cin and Heath were street urchins in District 17 before Zoey mated Dominic. They lived on dumpster food and by their wits against any danger. Lorenzo started hanging out with them, and Zoey tried her best to watch out for them."

"Mafia turning to charity."

"A bit. These kids, though, weren't here to just take. Cin is the one who makes most of the jewelry the women of Encantado are wearing right now, and Lorenzo has been working on Pack finances to keep our money clean. They are invaluable."

"They are pups."

Yes, he was right. Every wolf who'd struggled, who lived by the Code, saw these kids as designers of their own fates. They'd beaten the odds, remained true, and carved out their place in the pack without even being able to shift. Other than Zoey, Kalinda, and Silva, they were the only non-shifter inhabitants of Lombardi Pack land. The placement of their people so close to the inner sanctum was symbolic of what they'd done. The young couple lived a stone's throw away from Giuliana, and their home had been built by the wolves to suit them.

Just like any member of the pack.

They wanted for nothing, would be provided every wish they could ever want, and all they asked was to be family. It was humbling, that sort of love. That sort of loyalty.

It made it all the harder for Giuliana to knock.

But she'd honor who they were.

Cin, her dark-pink bob framing her chin, answered by the time Giuliana hit the door the third time. She wore red leggings and a white shirt cut to hang off her shoulders. Her earrings were little lanterns hanging from the lobes. She'd changed so much from the skinny girl with the spikey blue hair.

"Did you find him?"

"May I come in?"

"Oh … oh gods, Giuls, no."

Cin was the only person in the world who dared to call Giuliana by a nickname and live, but she crumpled now. Giuliana grabbed her before her knees could hit the floor, lifting the young woman off her feet and carrying her farther into the home. Cin curled into her, fisting her shirt as she sobbed.

Giuliana believed Cin may have loved Heath, in her own way. In the way friends can fall in love slowly and never realize it. In the way you wake up one morning and realize you can't be without the other. But Lorenzo had appeared and changed everything—some inferno she couldn't get free of—and she found something real.

It wasn't easy on any of them. Life was never easy, but they'd found a way, and Heath stayed beside them.

More than anything, it pissed Giuliana off because the wolves who'd taken him from this group had made Cin and Lorenzo believe Heath had done it on his own.

Cin exhaled roughly, sucking in her tears as Giuliana lowered her to her bright-pink couch and sat beside her.

"Where is Lorenzo?"

As if Giuliana summoned had him, Lorenzo walked through the door and slipped a gun from his waist before setting it on a table, all without looking up. It was on the tip of Giuliana's tongue to chastise him about being unaware of his surroundings when his gaze met hers.

He'd been absolutely aware someone was in his home before he entered, and he'd also assumed it was a friend. The darkness in his gaze disappeared as he closed his eyes and took a deep breath.

"Where is the body?"

In that moment, she couldn't have been prouder of a young pack member finding his way. He may have been clumsy and not battle-hardened. He may have been afraid of Dominic's Alpha call, as he wasn't shifter and couldn't fight on the same grounds, but he was a member of the Lombardi, and it showed.

"We don't have it," Giuliana answered.

"Is it retrievable?"

"I would have brought him home."

Lorenzo nodded and crossed from the foyer to where Cin wept quietly in a pillow. He pulled her into his arms and sat so she could balance on his lap and tuck her face into his neck. His large hand soothed her with easy, soft strokes down her spine.

He pressed his lips to her ear. "Why don't you go work on the piece for Zoey?"

He was quiet— not enough her shifter hearing couldn't pick it up—but Giuliana acted like she didn't hear it anyway.

"I can't work right now."

"This is the best time for you to work. You know that. How much did you make when Heath went missing?"

What a difference a disappearance had made. It surprised her, really. This wasn't the young boy shaking with fear when he'd come to Kalinda and she'd been called to answer his fear Heath had been taken. This wasn't the Lorenzo she remembered wanting to swallow his tongue when he thought Heath would be killed.

Growing up fast always hurt the most, but it sometimes brought steel where weaker wood had been.

Cin nodded and got up. "I'll talk to you later?"

The question was directed at Lorenzo, and Giuliana understood what Cin was really saying. *You'll tell me what you can, right?*

"Yeah, babe. Always."

Assurance taken, Cin left the room with only a backward glance in Giuliana's direction. After a moment, Lorenzo sighed. "Tell me."

"We found his blood in a clearing in the Greenwald and the scent of wolves. I didn't find his body, but there was enough there to tell me he didn't make it."

Lorenzo swallowed before raking his hands through his dark hair. "The wolves weren't … ours?"

Giuliana shook her head. "No. Dominic never gave the order to execute him. He kept his word on finding him first and questioning him." She reached out and touched his knee. "There is more."

Pasquale shifted, and Giuliana went quiet. This was his part of it to tell. "They were Bianchi."

Lorenzo and Pasquale were on their feet, Pasquale beating Lorenzo to his gun at the door.

"*Your* people?"

Lorenzo may have not made it to his weapon, but he made up for it in fury. He balled his fist and swung at Pasquale's face. The wolf dodged the blow enough he wouldn't break Lorenzo's fingers, but he took the brunt of it.

"Yes."

"And you come into *my* home?"

Giuliana rose, but she stopped when Pasquale shook his head. "You know what happened with Primo and Dominic."

Lorenzo, huffing, faced Pasquale. "Of course."

"Then you know not all of my people joined Lombardi." Pasquale looked to Giuliana.

"The sect that attacked Heath were Bianchi but not really part of the pack."

Lorenzo turned to her, but he backed up in a way he'd still be able to see Pasquale and his weapon.

Good pup.

"How is that possible? I didn't think wolves did that."

"And yet you struck out at a Lombardi because of his previous affiliation. If you can do it, why can't we?"

She lifted one brow, and Lorenzo only shook his head before coming to sit back down. Pasquale leaned against the door.

Smart wolf.

"Many don't know what I'm about to tell you, and it doesn't leave this room."

Translation: this part isn't for Cin.

Lorenzo nodded, and Giuliana continued. "There are wolves who are more like mercenaries. Primo hired them to bolster his strength against Arturo and Dominic. It was these wolves who attacked Heath."

"Why?"

"That's what we want to find out, and we *will* find out, Lorenzo. We swear it."

"I know. Just … give us some time. He was my best friend … and …" Lorenzo looked to where Cin had gone. "And maybe more for her. We never spoke about it, but we always knew. It was always there."

"Did Heath ever say anything?"

"Never. I think he knew how she felt, but he just kept them as friends. And when I came around, I think he was relieved. I didn't notice it at first, and he stayed away at the end, but I think he was trying to give time for that part in her heart to die."

The wolf part of her understood, and she sniffed, just to make sure her nose hadn't lied to her about Lorenzo just being a low-level mage. She cut her eyes at Pasquale.

You don't smell wolf on him, do you?

No. Just pain and anger. He's got magic, for sure.

She thought so. Still, Lorenzo had a very wolf way of dealing with Cin's feelings for Heath. Not that many did it anymore, but at one time, females in packs took on more than one mate because they were scarcer. The main mate was bonded to them, but they could accept other pack members to continue bloodlines. Lorenzo reminded her of that.

"Take care of her. As soon as I know more, you'll be the first I contact. For now, we have to try to get what information we can from other packs. There is so little known about this group."

Lorenzo perked up. "What's their name? I may be able to get somethings together."

Giuliana looked to Pasquale before closing her eyes and covering her ears. She was *not* about to lose her shit at the mention of them. After a moment, Pasquale's voice filled her head.

Coast is clear. I've also explained a bit of your reaction to the word so he knows not to say it directly.

Thank you.

She opened her eyes and lowered her hands to her lap. She'd have to deal with her memories at some point, but for now, her only duty was being there for Lorenzo.

"I'll see what I can find. We're going to the Bianchi wolves next to see what some of them may know about the group of men around Primo."

Lorenzo's dark eyes lifted to Pasquale's face. "What do *you* know about them?"

"Only that they existed and he used them for his most deadly missions. He liked to keep them away from the pack, of course."

Do you mean away from you?

Yes. I don't think he wanted me to have a chance to use them against him if I could afford more than him.

What wolves would know more?

Pasquale sighed in her head.

Fabiana, I'm guessing.

Yes. I don't know how much he let her see, but she was always right at his side so he could keep an eye on her. She knows more than she realizes.

We go to her house next.

Mine.

She growled at that and had to catch herself. Fabiana was his *sister.* "I'll be back, Lorenzo."

"Yeah, and I'll get to work. It's better than wallowing in the darkness."

"Revenge usually helps with that."

The emptiness in Lorenzo's gaze plastered her heart to the floor. "I hope so, Giuliana. I fucking hope so."

Pasquale's home was on the edge of Pack lands, closer to the outer wall border, but it still didn't take them longer than twenty or so minutes to get there at a full-out run, cutting through backyards as they went. The Bian—*former* Bianchi, she corrected herself—moved out of their way quickly when they saw them coming. Some stifled bows in Pasquale's direction when they saw her.

They protect him. She wouldn't have noticed the bows if she hadn't been looking for it since she knew he was Alpha material. But with the knowledge, she was seeing him in new light. He slowed down near older wolves and gave them a word before continuing. Or he let children race him for a few minutes before they gave up and his laughter trickled over her.

They may have been on a mission, but he took time out for them.

His home, like Dominic's, was in the center of the space allotted them, and the other wolves milled around in his front yard. Giuliana lifted a brow when they came to a stop.

Pasquale stood tall, letting his Alpha call unfurl. *Thank you.*

The wolves there stretched before loping away in different directions.

"They listen to you."

"Yes."

"As their Alpha."

"Yes."

Okay. Back to not giving much in response, so she went quiet.

"I'm sorry. Yes. They answer my Alpha call, and I put them on protecting her while I was gone. I don't do it often, but I had to release them or they wouldn't leave. Since you know what I am …"

He'd done it in front of her. She stepped up and took his hand. A smaller wolf that hadn't gotten all the way to its home blinked at the motion.

Pasquale's Alpha call whipped out, this time with deadly precision and warning. It slid over her skin like a caress, but she was aware others wouldn't have felt what she did.

Mate.

One after another, wolves outside and in their homes lifted their heads in a howl of acknowledgment. Pasquale held on for a few beats more before letting his power fade away.

"Well, that was a pissing contest moment."

"I'm perfectly okay with that assessment. None of the men here need to get it in their head they could meld with Lombardi in other ways."

Giuliana gasped. "Are you jealous?"

"Territorial."

She rolled her eyes. "That's jealous in new-age language to try to cover it up. I can run around naked if I felt—"

Pasquale was in her face, teeth bared, and a growl rumbling before she could finish the sentence. "I'll gut anyone who sees you. Go ahead, play with fire."

No, she didn't think she would. The threat was enough to get Pasquale bothered in ways she sort of wished they had time to explore. He was holding himself in check, but she wondered if he'd have shown her just how he was the only one who'd ever see her naked again if they'd been behind closed doors when she made the offhanded remark.

"Am I supposed to never have sex again?"

I mean, since we aren't claiming each other.

This time, Pasquale didn't hesitate to put his hands on her. His heated palms burned her forearms as he curled his fingers around her arm. A brand. A mark. He pulled her against his body until their breaths mingled between them and his lips were only an inch away from hers.

"Who ever said I don't plan on meeting your every need? Pack business first, but my business later."

Giuliana swallowed against the sudden aching need spreading through her. Okay, so she'd needed a bit of distraction after the heaviness inside of Lorenzo's home, and sometimes laughter could really hit the spot. But she was finding desire burned so much hotter. She wanted to see, to have him take her, to feel what it meant to be claimed by her mate.

It was dangerous.

It could fuck them up.

But here, among his people, he wouldn't have to risk anything if his Alpha power leaked out. If they pushed the boundaries and just didn't let him mark her as his with the mating bite. If …

She wanted to see if they could.

"Can you hold off the bite?"

Pasquale's eyes glittered. "The better question is, would you want me to?"

"Pasquale …"

"For you, I would. And for you, I'd give it when you asked."

He'd let her control the fate. Give her the freedom of choice.

"But you have to understand, Giuliana. The way I'd love you may make you more afraid than ever to accept me."

She wasn't so sure. And no matter how many times he tried to warn her away—and she could appreciate him fighting for her—he gave her something she craved more than anything.

The freedom to choose.

"Pack business first," she agreed.

His gazed stayed riveted on her for a heartbeat before he backed away and headed to his door. She took a steadying breath, smelling him everywhere. The snow. The deep earth. But under it, just barely, was that mark of fresh flowers, the feminine scent she'd picked up before.

Fabiana.

She was here enough to permeate the space with her smell.

You could mark it.

I'm not going to go around pissing on his things.

Why not?

Because that's gross.

Would get her scent out of here. Just saying.

She ignored her wolf.

Red, thank you very much,

Fine. She ignored *Red* and followed Pasquale into the house. Fabiana, all willowy and dark hair, was standing at the bottom of the stairs as soon as they entered. She had on a pretty, white summer dress that fluttered in the breeze from outside. It should have been someone's marketing photo; it was so perfect. *She* was perfect.

Something about Fabiana said to protect her, to wrap her in gauze and save her from the hell of the world. The gentle way Pasquale took Fabiana into his arms and hugged her spoke of that.

Giuliana had never been soft like that. Never been one to be protected because she couldn't protect herself. They'd done it because they thought it was best for her. She'd never been fragile. And sometimes, she worried her fight to be so strong and independent made her so she'd never be what men wanted.

Strong men, powerful men, wanted women who made them feel needed. Not women who'd rip off their balls for stepping the wrong way. Not women like Giuliana.

It's exactly what we want.

Snow. He'd spoken into her mind, and Giuliana's gaze met Pasquale's over Fabiana's head.

We hold her so we won't break her. We hold you because we know, even with all our strength, you're impossible to shatter. The snow is of home, but fire is in the heart.

She swallowed as Snow's words faded in her head.

Oh my gods … he is soooooooooooo going to get laid.

Way to ruin the moment, Red.

Only because your panties haven't hit the floor.

His sister is standing right there.

Audience!

Um, no.

Spoilsport. She'd run away anyway. You blow too hard and the girl would crumble.

She's not weak.

Giuliana was surprised at her own defense of Fabiana, but she wouldn't call her weak, not after what Pasquale had told her.

"Hello, Paz."

Paz? She calls him Paz? Mine!

Simmer down. I think the name is cute.

Diminutive for a diminutive woman.

Cut it out.

Her wolf only stuck her tongue out, obviously in a snit because she wasn't going to get some at the moment.

"We need to talk to you, Fabiana."

Fabiana ducked her head and hid her face in Pasquale's shoulder. "Am I about to get in trouble?"

Pasquale stepped back and held her arms, and Fabiana looked up at him. "No. Just need information to help with the missing pack member."

"Okay …" She peeked over at Giuliana. "You sure?"

"Yes, little one. Now, Giuliana, I'm going to say it."

With balled fists and determination not to let that singular world blow her to smithereens, she answered. "Go ahead."

Impossible to shatter.

Snow's words bolstered her.

"We need to know about the Renegades."

Run! Hide! The Renegades are coming.

Don't let the memories overtake you.

Impossible to shatter, Giuliana. Remember.

"They had been with … Primo—"

"She knows."

"With father, not long after he took over his pack. He was friends with one. Alexi."

Don't come out until I come for you.

"I don't remember Alexi."

"He stayed outside the compound. The Renegades stayed in Scorched Earth unless called for."

Heath's scent had been in that direction. How had they had traitors so close and never been aware?

"All the wolves are black as night, the men vicious and hard, better killers than anyone."

And it seemed the Lombardi Pack was going to war with them.

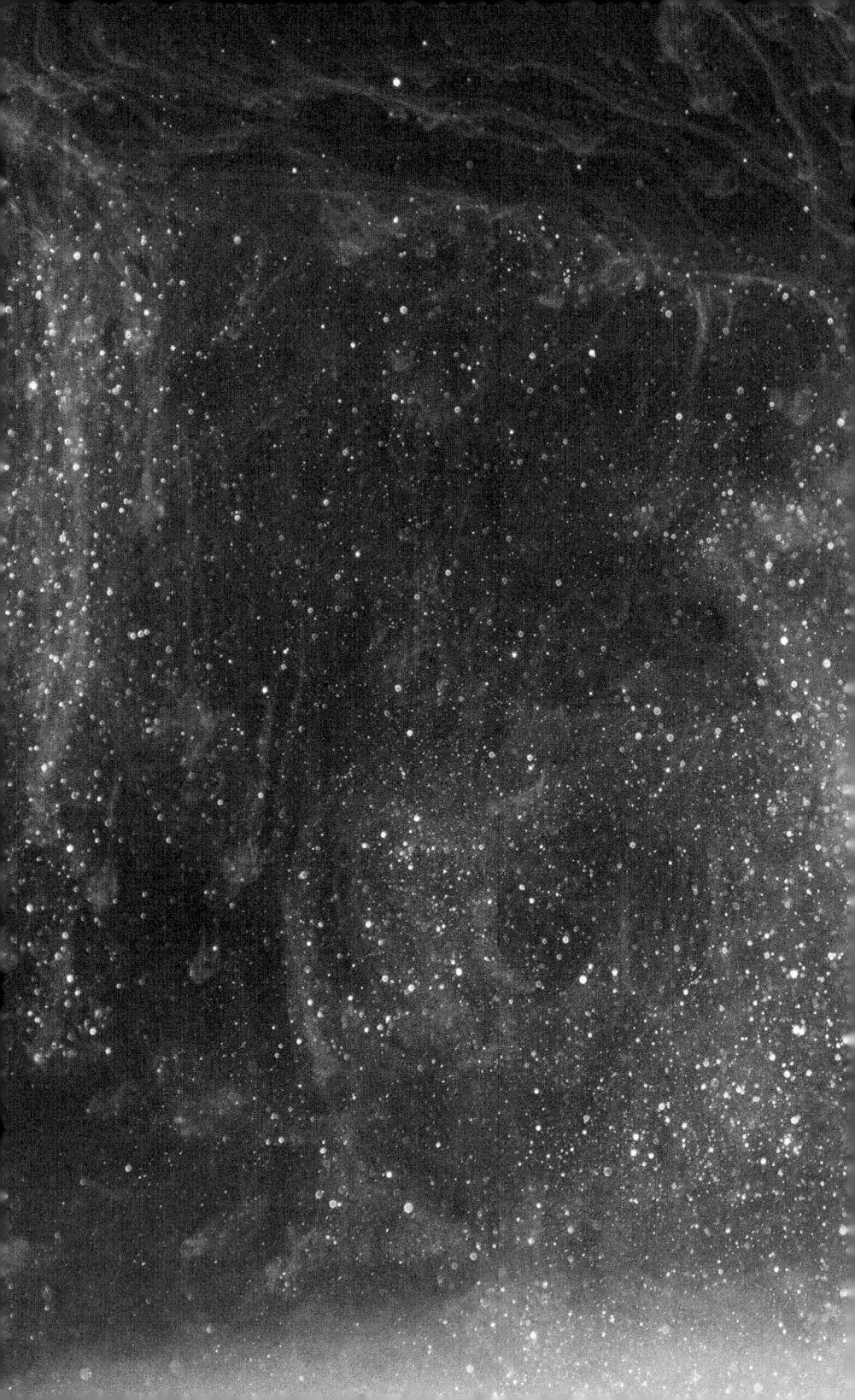

CHAPTER ELEVEN

If Silva never fucking opened her eyes again, she'd be thankful.

Problem with that, of course, was that life was a tenacious bitch and wouldn't let her give up, even when she really wanted to. No, that wasn't right. That was the pain talking. She *had* to get up, or Kalinda wouldn't survive.

She started with her pinky. It seemed like a good idea, until flames streaked across her nerve endings and made her realize that maybe the little piggy cried all the fuck the way home because it *hurt*. She could barely catch her damn breath.

Her wings were nothing more than pathetic frazzled lumps of gossamer clinging to her back and she wanted to scream just attempting to unfurl them.

Silva never knew how much she'd missed flying until they'd sprung from her—thanks to Kalinda bringing her back from the brink of death. Before her chains broke, she hadn't remembered how powerful she was or that she could even fly. Now she knew she could, and the loss of them was like cutting off legs. Hot tears of anger and betrayal burned their way down her cheeks. They'd heal … maybe. If she got out of here first.

Kieran of the Shadow.

He knew who she was, and even how to target her. Fae, as a whole, had elements attached to their magic: fire, earth, air, water, and shadow. Shadow—deadly because it could mimic the others and was rare for their kind—was a bitch to deal with. Silva's magic was based on earth, from deep within the Earth's womb where precious metals stemmed from. She controlled silver, or to more aptly put it, she could harden her frame. It's what made her able to sustain most magics mages could use—outside of Kalinda, of course. She was badass. The weakness of it, though, was it could be formed. And what formed silver? Fire.

Fire was used to turn so many minerals and stones into something else entirely, like steel into sword, or coal into diamond. And since he'd known her name, her *real* one, he knew her power. Those of marked connection to an element gained a name tied to their gift.

Kieran was obviously an adept user of shadow.

Silva forced her eyes open and swallowed the answering pain that reverberated in her skull. Kalinda was gone, not dead, but gone. In a lightning-quick crash, fear swept over her.

She'd failed as a *Cosantiór* for Kalinda. She hadn't been strong enough to battle those coming for her and had been too assured in her power.

No mage could stand against a Fae of Silva's strength, not without serious help from higher levels. Not too many to be found in Encantado. It wasn't a boast, just simple truth.

Kieran was not supposed to be here.

A wave of dizziness threatened to take her back down on her knees, but Silva was determined to get to her feet. Kalinda was important to the magical world but not so much in the Fae world, outside of her connection to Silva. *That* would be worth falling all over themselves for. If they'd been in the Fae world, though, Kalinda would have been at the right hand of Silva in the throne room, their positions essentially reversed and Kalinda's connection to her protecting her from outside attack.

But they were in Encantado, somewhere Unseelie never should have fucking been.

She swayed, but at least she'd made it to standing without keeling over.

Score!

But where was Kalinda?

A glowing sheet of paper rested on Kalinda's destroyed desk, and Silva wanted to burn it to cinders. She knew without even reading what it said; it was from the Unseelie Fae.

Fucking bloodsuckers.

No, really. Daywalkers came from the Unseelie as mages came from the Seelie. It was a little-known fact—one Silva wouldn't be sharing with anyone. While she let the Lombardi in on a bit of Fae lore, some of the information was secret for a reason.

If daywalkers realized their gift was from the Fae and there were other applications of their feeding gift—as the Unseelie did already—things would go to shit.

One of them being the slip of parchment resting on Kalinda's desk. It was a way to sap Fae energy from another to ensure the information was seared in the intended's brain before it disintegrated. It was a rather nice way to also kill one, if set with a trap.

Silva had no doubt the parchment set out by Kieran would both feed from her and fuck her world up, especially how weak she was.

"Then that's the last resort."

But searching the room as painstakingly slow as she could move without puking turned up nothing. Of course, she already knew that. She sighed and approached the glowing paper.

"He's so fucking dead. I swear by The Fates."

The Fates gave no sign they'd heard her, and she wasn't so sure those mythical controllers of time still favored the Fae anymore, but she prayed anyway. The document was blank as her hands hovered over it, and she bit her lip.

"You're really going to make me touch this."

The last thing she remembered was enough fire to sap all the oxygen out the room, and Kalinda's screams melding with her own. She had no doubt Kieran wanted something from Silva, and that's the only reason Kalinda was still alive—for now.

"Can't get shit from me if I'm dead though."

It wasn't a comfort, but she had to make herself believe. Had to trust she wouldn't face the end and leave the Lombardi without Kalinda.

As much as she picked at the wolves, they'd become family in a short time. Watching Zoey and Kalinda with their mates, the way the pack was together as one unit, was so different than her court.

That was paved with blood and intrigue, like any other place, but the ones most ready to stab you in the back were family. Whole houses rose and fell for the chance to gain power. Silva had been … no different.

She sucked in a breath, not wanting to think of everything she'd lost.

The sister she'd never see again.

Silva had been stupid … so stupid, and time in the human world without memories made the hurt brand-new.

To escape the emotional pain of her memories, she grasped the *zethper*—finally calling it by name.

Cold spread through her, rolling over her flesh and leaving numbness behind. It was better than the pain, better than struggling for air. But as it reached her diaphragm, she realized she spoke too soon. It wasn't numbing; it was paralyzing!

She couldn't breathe. Her lungs wouldn't inflate, and she crumpled to the ground.

Come to Scorched Earth, where I have your ward. But come soon, and alone. She won't survive if you don't.

The power of the *zethper* kept her bound, winding around her windpipe and seizing until she flopped on the floor, a fish out of water. Every cell inside her strained for oxygen, to *live*. The urge to claw at her throat, at the invisible hand holding her in a vise grip battered at her brain, but she couldn't fucking move.

It's a sick feeling when the head is there, the soul is screaming, but the body slowly fades away.

Live, Silva. For Kalinda.

Suddenly, the lights faded, the world shrank, and she was hovering above herself.

You look like shit, Silva. Total shit.

And she did. Her wings were nothing but gnarled and twisted stumps out her back, her sundress was in tatters, showing blackened skin everywhere. Even her lips were blue from lack of air, and her eyes were bloodshot.

Not yet.

She—well, spirit her, because physically, she was screwed—flipped over and a bright white light glittered.

I'm not ready to die, thank you. No crossing over the rainbow bridge and frolicking in the tulips for me, thank you.

When did you begin to speak as such?

Her heart stuttered. That voice. *Asherah?*

Merry met, sister mine.

The joy of hearing that voice was splintered against the knowledge it was in the spirit realm. *I'm sorry I didn't find you in time.*

There is found, then there is found.

You speak in riddles still.

I ... cannot stay long. It is hard to hold this. But it is not over.

I'm sorry. For everything.

Forgiveness was given long ago. It is nigh time the Queen step forward. May your days be long, sister.

She didn't get a chance to respond. The light slammed into her, forcing her back into agony and fire. She screamed, her cells opening to depleted oxygen, her skin sizzling as the burns faded enough to move.

One day, I shall hold you close once more. One day.

Her sister's parting words were all that was left of the connection before Silva opened her eyes once more. She was back on the ground, but a subtle flutter grabbed her attention. Her wings. They were healed. She may not be back to heavy hitter, but at least they'd carry her to where she needed to go.

Forcing herself up on her knees, she slapped them open and sped out the door.

Wait for me, Kalinda.

By the time Silva reached the edges of Lombardi Pack lands she could barely see straight.

A wolf called to her in greeting, used to seeing her travel this way with Kalinda if they wanted to get home faster. This time, she didn't stop; she couldn't afford to. The only wolf she was concerned with was Romano. If she could make it to him, he'd get the troops ready. *She* may not be able to choose to bring others with her, as directed by the *zethper*, but that didn't mean *he* couldn't.

And she needed help to heal. There was no way she could kick ass when she was still ready to keel over.

Romano's home was within sight, and she forced herself to slow down enough for as easy a landing she could muster.

"Romano!"

Her holler was made stronger by what meager power she had left. And the wolf, Fates save the bastard, ran out of his home, searching for her. Without any grace, she fell into his arms.

"Nice catch."

"What the hell happened?"

"Right to business. My sort of man. We need Zahara."

"I'll get her ... where is Kalinda?"

Silva swallowed. "Taken."

Three seconds. He was still for three whole seconds before he tucked her closer to his chest and ran. His harsh grip stung her burned flesh, but she didn't complain. This was Kalinda's mate, and Silva had failed him. He deserved his pound of flesh, no matter how he took it.

Romano moved fast enough he had to slide to a stop in front of Dominic's home before bounding up the stairs.

"Alpha!"

There was bellowing and scampering claws. Zoey hollered something about not a good time, but Romano wouldn't be deterred.

"It's Kalinda!"

The front door swung open, and Silva got a full view of Dominic's broad shoulders and bare chest before she caught the tail end of a decidedly naked Zoey ducking through a door.

"What is it?"

"Kalinda has been taken."

The world turned into a bunch of too-fast questions, calls for Zahara, and Silva finding herself laid out on a chaise in the main living room with Zoey running her fingers through Silva's hair.

"You're so burned."

Zoey's tearful observation made Silva's throat thick with sadness. "It was worse, but I was able to heal a bit to get here. Doesn't hurt as bad as it looks."

Zoey's look told Silva she didn't believe her but she didn't argue out loud.

"Zahara is on her way."

Silva forced herself to turn her head and face Romano. He looked how she felt: out of sorts, his hair standing on end, and ready to kill the nearest thing he was directed at.

She could get behind all of that.

"I'm sorry."

He shook his head. "You've never backed down from a fight. If you look like this, it had to be bad. Who took her?"

Silva took a deep breath. This was going to fucking *suck*. "And Unseelie Fae named Kieran of the Shadow."

"Come again?"

She explained as best she could about what happened. At the mention of the wolves, Dominic grabbed his phone and dialed quickly.

"It has to be The Renegades. Pasquale should recognize their scent if they are the same ones who killed Heath."

"Heath's dead?"

The world was going to fucking shit. And Kalinda was not going to be happy to find out this information.

"We believe so, and there were wolves involved. If these are the same wolves, this is personal. They are attacking the pack."

"I think I may be the reason."

Dominic stated at her. "Explain."

"The Unseelie and Seelie have never seen eye to eye. They are the dark Fae, for lack of a better word, always prone to cruelty and destruction. I can't ignore this is happening after I came into my power, or the fact he wants me to go there alone to get Kalinda."

"All this to take you out?"

Silva shrugged ... and hissed. That *hurt*. "I'm not just a Fae, remember? It could be more to do with my ruling House. But I can't be sure. Nothing is certain with the Unseelie. It could be on a fucking whim, and you all just got away."

"Some whim."

"Court intrigue where I'm from is deadly."

Dominic took that information and answered the door when someone knocked. Zahara breezed in, her face paint bright white against her skin. Thanks to Kalinda, Silva knew just who Rihanna was, and she was struck as how much the witch doctor looked like the celebrity. Even weirder when she realized she was Dominic's grandmother and probably just younger than Silva.

"I thought it was the baby, but I see it's the Fae chile. What you go and do to yourself, yeah?"

"Got my ass kicked."

Zahara snorted. "Understatement." But then she froze. "Fae."

Silva frowned. "Um, yeah. But you knew that."

"Not you, silly girl. The magic on you. Dark fire burned you."

Ah. The witch doctor knew way too much. "Yes."

Seeming to take her cue not to say anything more, Zahara approached Silva. "Zoey, I need you out of here. Can't have anything rebounding to the baby."

"Silva doesn't need to be alone."

"You're a sweet chile, but my great-grandbaby needs protection. I will heal the Fae Queen."

Zahara took Zoey's place at Silva's head as Dominic escorted his mate from the room. Romano stayed at Silva's side, gripping her hand in his.

"Take what you need from me," he whispered.

Silva had never seen Romano so serious unless Kalinda was involved. It warmed her, his presence beside her, his loyalty.

This was what family looked like, and Silva wouldn't lose any of them.

"I promise, I'll get her back."

"Not alone."

Silva nodded and let Zahara work. Her warm power slipped around Silva, soothing the burning. Pasquale came in and took one sniff of the room before nodding at Romano and leaving.

"The same wolves?"

"Yes. The same fucking *dead* wolves."

Yeah, Silva could get behind all of that.

CHAPTER TWELVE

Fabiana was not what Giuliana thought she was.
It was … a lot to swallow. Instead of the vixen surrounded with adoring men addicted to her specific brand of sex-wrapped damsel in distress, Fabiana only seemed to gain confidence when she studied a subject.

Even now, she watched Pasquale and Giuliana discuss back and forth among their wolves. "You're talking to one another."

The statement made Giuliana pause. She wasn't sure how much she could share with Fabiana—even if she was Pasquale's sister.

She just wants to understand.

It still took some getting used to, hearing Snow's deep voice in her head. She could sense his care and protection for the female. It also made her hot.

Was she hurt?

The wolf hesitated for a moment. *More than she'll ever tell anyone.*

Giuliana could understand that. Some wounds, some fears, she had never been able to share, not even with Dominic as they grew up. Her past was muddled, and even thinking of the memories she was so afraid of made her want to climb out her skin.

Realizing this made it easier to answer Fabiana. "Yes. I'm not sure how we can, but somehow Snow and Red communicate and allow us to."

"Snow and Red?"

Giuliana rolled her eyes. "Snow is your brother's and Red is mine."

Snow snorted in her head, and the sound drizzled over her nerve endings, setting fire to her core. How the hell was that possible? Pasquale's voice, she could understand, but things were different with Snow.

Mate.

The possessive grumble made Giuliana's thighs clench. It took her a minute to realize Fabiana was talking again.

"You named your wolves."

"Actually, they named themselves."

How much do you like my voice, Giuliana?

Enough to want to jump and wrap her legs around Pasquale. Red howled her agreement, pushing against Giuliana's skin.

Stop it. Now's not the time, Red.

Make time.

We have a mission. Dominic—

No.

The annoying wolf pushed harder, canines exploding in Giuliana's mouth. She clenched her lips together to keep them from being exposed. What the hell was wrong with her?

That's enough.

He claimed you.

What?

Well, yeah ... sure, he'd made it very clear she was his mate in front of the other members of his pack. That was his wolf staking claim so another wouldn't test her. It was the way of the wolf. That shouldn't be making her wolf act like a total bitch now, however.

Now.

I said no.

Red thrashed in her rib cage, jerking Giuliana forward a step before she could catch herself.

Now!

"Interesting. If you have time—"

"We don't, little one. There's information we need to get to Dominic. But once we're finished, you can ask all the questions you'd like, okay?"

Pasquale was gentle, softer than Giuliana had ever seen. He handled Fabiana like fragile spun glass.

What were they talking about again?

You. Pasquale. Snow. Together. Fucking.

That was *not* what they'd been talking about. Even if Giuliana couldn't keep up with the conversation anymore, she knew that.

Fabiana nodded, a frown lowering the tips of her lips. "I think you need to help her."

"What?"

"Your mate."

Pasquale's gaze swung to Giuliana, and she bit her lip against the answering heat licking between her legs. Red was driving her insane, and this was not the time for this shit. But the more Giuliana stared at him, the more she couldn't deny she wanted more.

Giuliana?

She couldn't answer him. Red was too loud, burning with need for her mate. Red didn't care that this wasn't the time. That neither Pasquale nor Giuliana hadn't come to this point.

No, all Red wanted was her mate.

I can't stop her.

What do you need?

You… Giuliana swallowed, afraid of what it would mean if she let her wolf take over. But she couldn't fight Red.

Snow?

She's going into mating heat.

That only happens with … Fuck!

Giuliana didn't know what they meant. *Mating heat? That isn't a thing for wolves, only the feline shifters.*

Not exactly. Out loud, Pasquale addressed Fabiana. "What did father tell you about mating heat?"

Fabiana frowned harder before understanding lit her gaze. "Mating heat only happens with Alpha pairings. It forces the couple to bond the longer their wolves are around each other. He'd hoped it would happen between me," she cringed, "and Dominic."

"Any way to stop it?"

Giuliana could be thankful he wanted to make this better for her, truly. But Red turned into a screaming and snarling fucking banshee the minute the words left Pasquale's mouth.

Mine!

Our Alpha demands—

Pasquale *is our Alpha.*

Giuliana could *sense* power rolling off Snow. She didn't know if he reacted to Red's affirmation, or if he was in the throes of the heat himself.

"Take your mate, brother."

Pasquale shook his head. "Not like this."

"You may not have a choice."

His eyes were sad when he looked at Giuliana. *I'm sorry.*

The wolves didn't care, and the more Red fought, the less Giuliana cared either. Her body was on fire, smoldering, muscles twitching with need. She'd fucking rip off Red's head later, but right now, she needed Pasquale.

Help me.

Even in her mind, her voice was angry and afraid.

I will. Trust me through the fear.

She could trust him, but mating meant a cage she wasn't prepared for. She didn't want to face what it would mean, the freedom she'd lose. And she didn't forget he'd warned her about how being with him would be.

That the things he needed would terrify her.

"Fabiana, go home. I've called a wolf for you and they'll escort you. I'll let you know when you can come back."

"Yes, Alpha."

Fabiana stepped gingerly away from Pasquale and gave a wide berth around Giuliana. Not the best way to meet her under different circumstances.

Pasquale never took his eyes off Giuliana, and the silence stretched, only broken by Fabiana opening and closing the door behind her.

"Are you sure?"

Mine!

Red's cry only made Giuliana struggle to stay standing.

"I don't have a choice."

"There is always a choice, Giuliana. Our wolves can't force what we don't want. Even if I have to separate us until this fades, I will. For you."

It always came down to this ... a moment, a choice. Pasquale or agony. Freedom or chains. Control or loss.

Red, don't do this.

It's for your own good.

It was all the warning she got before every cell in her body twisted, rearranging and morphing rapidly back and forth between wolf and human. The fluctuation muddled her brain, ripped away any coherent thought except to bed Pasquale.

"They don't control us. Make your choice."

His dark gaze captured hers. A demand. Pure will. Giuliana clung to that rock in the torrent of desire spinning around her. He was her anchor, her calm. The magnet on which her needle spun and gave direction.

"Yes," she whispered.

Pasquale stood tall, staring at her, seeing through her. His Alpha power curled out from him, a lazy show of force.

"Come here, Giuliana."

Her feet carried her to his side before she even knew she'd moved. His brand of power wrapped around her, caressed her heated skin.

"Strip."

It was an order, one she couldn't deny, couldn't fight. His face was hard, a muscle ticking in his jawline as he watched her.

She pulled her shirt over her head, exposing the black lace of her bra to his gaze. It was a physical touch, the way he looked at her. Her nipples hardened to pebbles, and she popped the back of the elastic to free her aching flesh.

"Faster."

Silken straps from her bra slid down her arms and fell to the floor with a delicate pat as she reached for her belt. Her fingers were numb, clumsy with craving. Somehow, she got her pants undone and kicked them down her legs.

She'd forgotten her boots.

She stood bare to him but locked at her ankles. He only lifted an eyebrow at her, unmoving, and a wave of embarrassment washed over her.

You are beautiful in every way.

Snow's voice was threaded with Pasquale's in assurance. But the threat, his command, was still there. Her hands worked hard to remove her boots and socks before she stepped out of her pants and underwear.

Pasquale studied her in silence, walking around her body to stand behind her. She could feel him there, pushing her, daring her to move a muscle.

"You will do everything I say, Giuliana. Everything. Do you understand?"

"Yes," she hissed.

"So good."

Hot hands glided over the curve of her ass, imprinting his touch on her skin. He spread the cheeks before lowering them, testing their firmness. Then he slicked his way over the front of her thighs. The motion brought him closer to her, his rough clothing rubbing against her back. The contrast was a spark dancing on the edge.

"Sometimes, you need a cage to be free, Giuliana. I'll show you what that means."

Pasquale lifted her into his powerful arms and stalked up his stairs. She didn't get to see much of his décor, not with him moving so fast. They entered a dark room, and she only got the impression of blues, whites, and black before he tossed her onto the bed.

Her breasts jerked with the fall, and his gaze followed the movement.

"Fuck, you're so perfect."

His words were guttural, a praise, a plea. Slowly, he peeled his clothing off, exposing a chiseled chest and abs, narrow waist, and a cock standing thicker and longer than Giuliana had ever risked taking. She was by no imagination a virgin, but sex for her had been quick and fast in the desperate moments she'd been able to flee from under Arturo's watchful eye.

Pasquale was not a man to be rushed or hidden away. Naked and in control, he traced a free hand down over her neck and between her breasts. Giuliana's breath came hot and fast, puffing over his chin as he caressed her.

"Don't think. Don't fight. Just feel. Let me take care of you as no one has before."

"I'm afraid."

"Of what?"

"Needing this."

"And need, for you, is a cage."

Giuliana nodded.

"I will take pleasure from your body and give you so much you'll want to run away. I'm going to demand it, Giuliana. And you can fear it, but don't run."

"Every man in my life wants to control me."

"Yes, except for me. I want you to *give* me control."

"That's the same thing."

"Oh, it's very different. Let me show you."

Giuliana bit her lip as Pasquale slipped his hand over her left breast. Her nipple pressed hard against his skin. She may have been afraid, but she wanted his touch.

His other fingers snaked around her right breast and nuzzled the flesh. The faint scent of snow wafted off him, and under it a warmer, spicier smell that belonged just to him. He buried his nose in her chest, inhaling deeply.

My scent does the same for him.

The sudden understanding blasted through her. She wanted a taste. She wanted to see him hover over her as he pounded inside. His tongue slid over her skin, mirroring her need. He licked his way to her nipple, sucking her inside his mouth. With each pass of his tongue, Giuliana grunted, her body tightening like a bow string.

Still sucking, he played with her other one. Pasquale pulled on her harder, tightening her nipple until he released it with a *pop*.

"One more," he whispered against her other nipple.

He gave it the same treatment, pulling on her, his fingertips dancing over skin. She couldn't fight the moan slipping between her lips. Or the harsh hiss cutting through the sounds of him pleasuring her. The hard, wet tip of his cock traced a path over her belly.

She shifted, wanting him closer, and he stopped everything, holding her down with one spread hand between her breasts.

"I said let me."

He was so strong, and that one insistent push made her freeze on the bed. His eyes dared her to challenge, to give him a fight, and something darker swelled inside her. If he wanted it, he'd have to take it. He'd have to *earn* her submission.

She bucked against him, and he smiled.

What the fuck was wrong with her? It shouldn't be like this. She shouldn't want him to be rougher, more demanding, stronger against her. She should have been running for the hills to get away from it. Instead she wrestled him, twisting and turning to gather purchase. She needed leverage to flip him.

She'd never been with anyone like this.

Never wanted to fight.

She'd always wanted to find a man who could handle her strength and match her.

Pasquale lifted her into the air, even as she angled a kick at his face. He slammed her back down. It zapped the air out of her lungs, sending her head spinning before he forced his way between her legs.

Pinned there, every emotion swelled within her. Giuliana knew her expression was a blend of anger, fear, and fragile need.

I don't want to love this, to come alive under his hands. To prove I crave the very control I've been running from. But she did. Tossing her head back, she opened to his rough touch.

Pasquale reached between her legs and circled his finger around her clit. This should have scared her. It should have made her hate him and want to fight against what he was taking from her.

But it didn't.

Each swipe of his finger pushed the nub of her clit out of its protective little hood.

"Let's see how you fly, Giuliana."

Pasquale slap her clit—hard. She screamed, shockwaves going through her. He slapped her again, this time pressing his fingers into her at the end. It was pain. It was pleasure. It was a roar building in her head. Stinging electrical currents of twisted need destroyed everything she thought she knew about touch. About sex. About mating.

Pasquale shattered her and put her back together in a haphazard mess of craving. He worked her clit more as her pussy warmed under him, growing slick.

Warmth spread over her skin, and her toes curled.

More. She needed more.

Of him. Of the edge of pain. Of the pleasure. *Him.*

Her gaze met his just as he slapped once more. With gritted teeth, her fingers white from her clenched fists, and her hair plastered to her face, she took what he gave her.

"Look how strong you are, Giuliana. Look what you can take. And look how your pleasure is all I'll ever want."

Pasquale helped her lift her head to peer down her body. His cock leaked pre-cum in a steady stream, covering her stomach and his shaft. It was nearly purple with need and jumped with each pulse of his heart.

"I *need* you. I want this. You've always thought you had to run away from being held to tightly. Maybe, mate, you just never met a man who'd hold you so strongly you never would fall. So that when you needed to break, you knew he'd be enough to pick up all the pieces. To protect what rests inside you … your heart."

She stared at him, said organ pounding. She'd never thought of it like that. Never believed she could view power as anything less than a way to control others.

But Pasquale wanted to free her.

He wanted to be the shield so she could be herself behind it.

And maybe, despite all the men around her, she needed that sort of strength.

He reached between them and jerked his cock with hard strokes. Pasquale paused, just a breath, taking in her body.

"Mine."

He pushed into her damp heat, and she clamped down around him like a vise.

All fucking mine.

His cock inside her was more than she ever could imagine. He was too large, too long, too *everything*. Her body bucked, recoiling to run away, but the burn of his touch also made her open up. She choked out a sob.

"Let me in."

Yes. He rocked back and forth. He had only slid in maybe an inch, but it stretched her until the burn spread. How could he get all the way inside? He'd ruin her. But he didn't have the same fears. His large hands found their way to her hips, holding her in place, and he slid a bit farther in.

"You can take it. You were made for me. I'm here."

Too much. Not enough.

Giuliana's body and mind were confused. She throbbed, twisting under him and breathing to take him deeper.

"Trust me."

Her frantic gaze met his. Pasquale released her hips with one hand and wrapped his fingers around her throat. Her pulse throbbed louder, echoing in her head.

"Feel how strong I am, baby. I won't let you get hurt. Never."

It shouldn't have worked, but it did. She gave in. To his control. To his insistent push inside her.

"Such a good girl."

More wetness slid from her, coating the hot skin where they joined, easing his path.

"Don't you want it all?"

Yes, please.

She moaned, reaching for his forearm and gripping it to anchor herself.

"Yes. All of you."

His smile was harsh and confident. A sexy twist of his lips. He pulled out a bit before slamming back in. In one hard jerk, he pushed all the way inside. She screamed. Each deep dig of his cock and his groin muscle rubbing against her tender clit served to sweeten the pleasure.

Everything spiraled, her chest heaving and oxygen freezing before going to her brain. Where before there was an edge of pain, now it had changed to a pulsing pleasure that hurt so good. Her nipples were aching points that accented each of his harsh thrusts.

She clenched her muscles inside, pulling him deeper. Needing more.

He was right … about it all.

The need.

The craving.

The chance to break free of her fear and let him change her.

She let him lead. Giuliana couldn't have compared his touch to anything she'd had before, or the late nights when she touched herself, seeking solace from the loneliness. He forced his hand between them, and she clenched her teeth as he stroked her clit. It stood out for him, hungry for more of his brand of electric sensation.

"It's there, Giuliana. Everything you've wanted. The thing you dreamed of and told no one. You're not alone anymore. Reach for it."

She sucked in a deep breath. Her dreams? She'd wanted love and passion, like any other woman. Companionship. Connection. And Pasquale was here, a force between her legs, showing her what it could be.

This whole mission with him had been a whirlwind. Each new thing she learned about his world pulled her in. Too fast, too easy. The ground had to fall out from under them sometime. But even as she thought it, she was doing what he said, focusing on his bruising fingers on her clit, the pound of his shaft within her. He wasn't gentle, and she realized she didn't want him to be.

He didn't treat her like she needed to be cared for because she was weak.

Impossible to shatter.

Yes. He recognized she was just as strong as him. That she could take anything he gave.

Giuliana would be the *only* woman in the world who could ever take him.

Pride and possessiveness swelled in her chest.

Mine!

Yes, yours.

A twist of gut-wrenching need echoed through their mental bond. Her toes tingled, and it snaked its way up over her calves and around her thighs. Warmth spread through her stomach, and she could just handle it, she could take one deep breath.

He pressed closer to her, his punishing thrusts battering her as his fingers begged for acceptance. And she was lost, torn between opposing sides. He was sweet and bitter, the knife plunging in and the safety shield of a bodyguard all wrapped into one.

Her clit throbbed with agony, but it sang with pleasure. Her nipples were tight with pinched pleasure, pulsing with each heartbeat. It sent his possession deeper into her skin. Too much. Everything about Pasquale was too much—from his touch to the remembered impressions on her skin.

The old her would have wanted to run away, to deny his possession, but he blasted her into new life, ripping from her any chances to hide.

Giuliana swallowed, and his vicious thrusts took her under. She was floundering, the softness of the cover underneath her a counterpoint to his burning haven.

Pasquale was an undertow, and she was drowning, exhilarated and terrified as she was battered under the water, a current pulling her to certain doom. His world would obliterate her old one. Remove any chance she'd ever be able to behave like she had before.

She didn't know which she was more afraid of: taking a leap of faith with him, or fighting to stay as she was.

His fingers dug into her thighs, pushing them as wide apart as they could go as he powered between her legs.

And her body crashed against the sharp rocks, breaking into little pieces. She'd had pleasure, those late nights with her hand working furiously under the covers. If she'd flown into the sky then, now she felt the weight of the earth press her toward the molten core.

Her chest seized, her throat worked, and she was breathless.

One false step and she'd die from it all.

Muscles locked, toes curled until they cramped, and her mouth open on a silent scream, she gave in to his ecstasy.

"Yes. You feel it. Right fucking there."

Giuliana followed him. His hips rolled against her, his cock thickening, and it only sent powerful vibrations over her ragged nerves. They melted, soldered together in this explosive destruction. And then he yelled, his cock jerking inside her and his seed branding her.

It tossed her, broke her to pieces and put them back together. The pleasure was blistering, rocking her core and forcing her body to curl up against him.

He held her through it, his teeth at her shoulder.

He didn't bite down enough to mark her, to complete what they'd begun, but the whispered promise was enough to soothe her wolf.

I will claim you when you aren't pushed by instinctual urges.

And he'd done what he'd promised—cared for her and showed her he was strong enough to do it.

This man, this wolf, had denied the call of the wild to mark her permanently as his even when she wouldn't have been able to stop it.

Mate.

Yes, in any way you need.

CHAPTER THIRTEEN

Kalinda hovered in magical quicksand. The murky gold slush allowed her to breathe, thank gods, but she couldn't do much but hover around it. No matter how much she tried to get to her feet, she only succeeded in twisting her dress around her legs and risking having an exposé moment for all to see.

Not her thing, and if her mate saw anyone checking her out there would be hell to pay.

Though, she should be grateful she was alive.

The burning flames from Kieran had burned hotter than hell but hadn't been meant to wound her. Instead, it messed with her mind and made her believe she was going to be a burnt mass for Romano to find. Kieran had also used the fire to shield them teleporting to another location.

Said location, she wasn't so sure of. It didn't look like any place she'd seen, and a lance of fear speared through her. Where was she? Had he taken her out of Encantado? Through the golden haze she was trapped within, large stones protruded through a blackened flat swathe of earth. It was sort of like … an arena, minus the bleachers or seating for visitors.

Beyond the arena was a forest of dead and white gnarled trees. Their branches had long ago given up producing anything living, and the vision of them was enough to make Kalinda look away.

Her captor walked around the flattened space—probably as large as half a football field—pointing at the ground and muttering. In the wake of where he stepped, white lines appeared on the floor, glowing brightly.

When he reached the end of his circle, he smiled. "*Falistinar.*"

The odd, sing-song language he spoke was the same as Silva. Kalinda hadn't heard much *Eldalisfae*—the language of the Fae—but she'd learned about it being with Silva and among the Mage Council. Much of Kalinda's power was rooted in the old connection mages used to have with the Fae court. Kalinda was the only known mage of old blood to revitalize that connection.

"I see you're awake."

No shit, Sherlock. "Where is Silva?"

"Niamh Danaan of the Silver is on her way here, I'd hope. For your sake. It's been two weeks."

Two weeks!

Romano would be losing his shit and probably destroying all of Encantado to find her.

"My mate—"

"Your *mate* has sent word my demands shall be met, but the object of my query was harmed enough to have to be healed properly. I suppose I shouldn't have destroyed her wings."

Silva would die without them, and Kalinda had no idea how she'd slept through two freaking weeks and wasn't aware.

"Don't worry, the *osraebrin* can sustain life for as long as it's active."

Not that she had any idea what the hell he was talking about, but she figured he talked about the glittery goo around her.

At least she wasn't dead. That had been Kalinda's greatest fear after the beating she'd taken and the fire had spread. "How do you know Silva?"

She knew Kieran, no matter how much he appeared like Silva, was not the same. His black eyes and darker visage were a dead giveaway. Still, he was Fae. Silva, as Queen, should have been untouchable for him.

Instead of answering Kalinda's questions, he stalked toward her. A portal opened behind him, but he never acknowledged it. Not that it mattered, since the Fae warriors and wolves he had with him in the Council mansion were the only ones that stepped through.

Oh good. We've got more assholes to deal with. Great.

Kieran sniffed the air, a very wolf-like move that surprised her. "I can smell her magic on you but no *wynathraeda*. She always was an overconfident queen."

Again, Kalinda was *really* tired of not knowing what was going on. "Taking me will bring Silva to your doorstep, but it will also bring my whole pack and the National Magic Council on you as well. It would be better to figure out what your demands are now."

Being in politics had, at least marginally, increased her diplomacy if nothing else. The sooner she got out of this, the better.

"Do you know the woman you follow so blindly?"

Kalinda shrugged, internally reaching for her magic. There was nothing. The inner spirits still didn't answer when she summoned them, and it frightened her. No one had ever been able to stop her power.

"It's this land. Outside of this area, there is a magic-dampening aura here."

He said outside the area, so she should be able to reach. But how did he know she was reaching?

Kieran rolled his eyes. "It's because I would be doing the same. But the binding spell you're in won't allow *any* magic to be used. Feel special. It cost a pretty penny to get that when I was back in my world, and I used it on you."

Except, she didn't feel special. She wanted out and wanted this over and done. "What do you want?"

"Ah, ah, ah. My question first. How well do you know Niamh?"

"Well, *Silva* is my best friend. Question answered. What. Do. You. Want?"

Kieran watched her for a moment, his head cocked to the side. "You believe that." He sighed. "She's a tyrant."

That was nothing like the Silva she knew. Sure, Silva had moments where Kalinda could see the regal part of her that demanded things, but it was usually to lower-ranking wolves where they all were treated as such, and it wasn't malicious. Most of the time, Silva was too busy enjoying posting embarrassing pictures of Encantado life on LeafBook to be worried about being cruel to anyone.

"That's not her."

"That's because you know a shadow of her. So can you truly call her your best friend?"

"I'm sure you're going to enlighten me otherwise."

Kieran chuckled. "I can see why she likes you. And maybe, if this were another time and place, I'd be softer with my methods, but I can't afford to. Niamh Danaan was exiled out of Seraph because her people couldn't stomach her."

"You're lying."

"Did you even wonder how a Fae Queen ended up with her power bound and living as a human? Come now, you can't be that naïve."

Kalinda *had* wondered, and there always seemed to be enough time to talk about it, but they never had. And the sadness on Silva's face when she recalled some of her memories made Kalinda hesitant to bring that sort of pain on her friend.

"Whoever she was then, she no longer is."

"Would you say that to a reformed murderer?"

No … she didn't think she could. Would anyone?

Maybe.

She caught a flash of reddish-black fur and her heart soared in her chest. A wolf was here, and not one of Kieran's—they were all accounted for at his side. But she didn't know the wolf. There was scarring along its muzzle and down under its chest, and it didn't seem to be particularly interested in her. Mostly, it seemed to be investigating all of them.

The wolf ducked back out of sight before Kalinda could try to get word to it. But Kieran was right in front of her now. The wolves he'd brought in sniffed the air in the direction the wolf had disappeared and rose to their feet. The largest wolf stepped forward out of the group, studying the forest with his muzzle in the air.

After a moment, he stepped back in line.

So a wolf they don't know either. If Kalinda saw it again, she'd have to try to see if it was friendly to the Moretti or Lombardi. If it wasn't but knew the Moonstone pack, she could at least reach out to Jeremiah. He was the liaison between the wolves and Mage Council, and she'd gotten to know him well since taking over. The Moonstone Pack may not fight outright but would in defense of Encantado.

For now, she had Kieran to face. "We're going around in circles. The Silva I know is my partner. That simple. So what do you want from her?"

"I want my life back. I want my history changed so I don't have to watch my friends die in the fucking gutter while that bitch queen sat on her throne and did nothing!"

The sky darkened, lightning streaking from cloud to cloud when Kieran yelled. Kalinda's eyes widened, but she couldn't move away in the magic bubble. She was stuck, trapped with no way to protect herself when he could control the very elements around them.

But ... he'd said Silva had done nothing. "I don't understand."

He looked at her, anger leeching out of him until all that remained was anger and loss. "In my world, there are those who are hated simply for being who they are. If you live in the country of your birth, it isn't so bad. But if you are unlucky enough to be born elsewhere, in places where your race has been nothing but captive all their lives, they hate you. The resent you for not being one of them. They are afraid of who you are. And yet ... we're the ones they force to do their work, to spew their hatred on, and use our bodies until we're shriveled up. Until we're too afraid to stand up."

She understood. Who *didn't* understand hatred between countries, races, or supernatural beings? The daywalkers hated the wolves. Humans hated mages. Wolves hated the feline shifters. There were those who didn't care for divides between the paranorms, but every group had their own prejudices and history between them to excuse their actions.

Kalinda had been working hard in Encantado to ease the burn of lower levels being tossed out of human society just because they had traces of magic. She'd lived in a world where she had to be a bit smarter and work harder than anyone else. And without anyone wanting to admit the reason ... she knew why.

So yes, she understood. Knew what that deep-seated pain felt like. Had tasted bitterness at times and joy at others, even with the gifted life she had when compared to others.

Torn between wanting to soothe the pain in his gaze and anger at his methods, she swallowed. "Why take me? This can't make your purpose any better."

"I took you because I've given up hope things will change. I tried to live a normal life, to leave it all behind, but it found me anyway. Silva showed up, her power reaching across all barriers, and it was enough to remind me you can't run from your past."

"But she won't come alone."

"It won't matter in the end. You see, there is something she's bound to. Something she won't be able to say no to. And you're the perfect leverage to ensure it."

This made no sense. While he may have known of Silva from her Fae heritage, he shouldn't have known her connection to Kalinda.

Not exactly.

Kalinda had to admit Silva was always with her. She was right beside Kalinda at her acceptance speech to the people of Encantado when she took office. Silva posted regularly on LeafBook. The whole of Encantado may not have been aware of *what* Silva was to Kalinda, but they at least could see how important they were to each other.

Their very open friendship had put Silva in danger, and from an angle none of them could foresee. Kalinda hadn't learned much about the Fae relations, figuring that world was forever closed off. Now she wished she'd pushed a bit more. That she'd asked Silva about it all and understood the truth.

It may be too late.

Another flash grabbed Kalinda's attention. This time, the wolf was closer, lifting its muzzle in Kalinda's direction for a moment before a howl ripped through the space. Kalinda shuddered at the sound.

With the shifters, she had learned to recognize a sense of humanity within them. This wolf had none. It was all predator. All power.

The wolves behind Kieran got to their feet, but the largest wolf once more stood to the front and stared down the wolf beside them.

"It's an animal, not shifter. Get back in line."

The larger beast growled at Kieran but pushed back. Its eyes never left the scarred wolf to Kalinda's side.

Where had the wolf come from?

Kalinda didn't remember there being wild wolves anywhere in Encantado. In fact, she didn't know too many animals that were native to the area. Anything that could walk on four legs could also walk on two when they chose. So it made no sense for there to be a lone wolf.

Without her magic, Kalinda couldn't reach out to read or get a sense of anything more though. She was trapped, much like a human, with no extra support. She didn't realize how much she'd come to rely on those gifts until she couldn't access them.

It was like being cut off from a limb.

"For what it's worth, I'm sorry."

"Then don't do this, Kieran."

He shook his head. "I don't have a choice. She deserves to die for what she did. And today, I will kill her."

"No!"

But Kieran wasn't listening. He'd already turned away. The portal he'd called before opened up again at the wave of one of his Fae, and he stepped inside. His men and the wolves he'd brought trailed in behind him.

When he looked to Kalinda, the rage and sorrow battled in his gaze.

He'd kill Silva because he had to.

And Kalinda would do everything she could to save her.

They were enemies by circumstance.

Life tended to give shit cards, didn't it?

CHAPTER FOURTEEN

All combatants to me!

Dominic's call blasted through Pasquale's head and made him shoot up from bed. Giuliana, a constant guest in his home, did the same. They'd barely gotten to sleep after meeting with the Boulder wolves about the Renegades.

Stuffing his legs into his pants, he surveyed Giuliana. She was still trembling, the force of her remembered memories from the night before still holding her in their grip. He hated they'd had to get out of bed so quickly after she'd finally fallen asleep. But they'd been tired from going after Kalinda until Silva completely healed. While Zahara had restored her skin and wings, internally, the magic that tore Silva to shreds had done insurmountable damage. And as a Fae, she didn't operate the same way a mage would under the witch doctor's care.

Silva's full recovery made them all pissed and edgy. Especially Romano. He'd been pacing the grounds, his rage and helplessness sparking a few attempts to go steal back his mate.

All stopped by Dominic, who knew going against enemies they weren't prepared for would be suicide. At least Kieran sent a daily proof-of-life photo directly to Romano's phone, but none of them knew how long that would last.

"You think she's ready to go now?"

Giuliana was dressed in her pants and tank top he'd become accustomed to her wearing. Part of him missed her designer gowns and flowing shirts when she was more relaxed. But they'd all been prepared to fight at a moment's notice.

"She has to be for him to call all combatants. We'll be moving out soon enough."

Giuliana nodded and headed to his door, but Pasquale stopped her. "Hey."

"I'm fine."

He pulled her into his arms. If he hadn't learned anything else in his time with her, he knew Giuliana was not *fine* when she used that word.

"Just focus on the mission."

"I'm trying. My dreams … they were …"

She let her voice fade, and Pasquale waited patiently for her to continue. She needed to get it out. She had to share what she was going through.

"They are getting longer, and more real."

"You said you wanted to remember your past, didn't you?"

"But it's all fear and blood. Someone keeps pushing me into a closet to hide, but I never get anything more than a sense of red hair before they're gone. I'm not closer to knowing who there are or what happened than when I started remembering."

"It will take time, and it will come. I will be here through it."

"I don't like not knowing who I am."

"You're Giuliana Moretti, niece of Arturo Moretti and Enforcer to Dominic Lombardi. You are my mate and the owner of Touch of Old. That's who you are."

Her gaze searched his for a moment. "You're right. I just wish I remembered who I had *been*."

"A step at a time. For now, we go to Dominic."

Alone, they didn't use the term Alpha for Dominic. Their wolves didn't want to seem to respect it, and it was easier not to fight against them. Pasquale still wasn't ready to continue and flow more into the Alpha world, but he'd take what steps he could.

A screech made him whirl around and face his mate once more, ready for battle. She was swiping at her arms like a crazy woman.

"What?"

She didn't answer him, stomping on the floor in a circle.

What is wrong?

Spider, Red answered.

A spider?

She's afraid of spiders.

Pasquale looked to the ground. The eight-legged creature was crawling away, nowhere near Giuliana. He swallowed a laugh, not wanting her to think he was picking on her. He made a big show of stepping on the spider, smashing it beneath his boot.

"It's dead, Giuliana. Look."

Her gaze was frantic, searching.

He lifted his foot and pointed. "See?"

She froze, her chest heaving. "Don't say another word."

"But it's—"

"Not one word."

Giuliana, we all fear something.

Yeah? I'm a wolf afraid of a bug.

Well, yeah. That was a bit odd. Especially as wolves normally lived in the woods. But she was also a person who had phobias. He could understand that.

"And I'm a wolf afraid to be in cars," he said allowed. "I suppose I'll be the one on bug duty."

She shivered. "Yeah. Anything that crawls that isn't an ant."

He didn't suppress his smile then. "Will I get a reward?"

"Sure, as long as you kill it."

He stood, waiting and expectant.

She frowned. "What?"

"I'm waiting."

"What? Now? Are you serious?"

He didn't move. He liked this side of her, a part of her that needed him, even if for something as small as killing her fear of a crawling insect.

After a moment, she sighed roughly. "Men."

Her heat seeped into his skin, her scent wrapping around his balls as she stepped into him. When her arms wrapped around his neck, he pulled her closer to his chest, crushing her breasts against him. The soft globes flattened under the pressure.

Silken lips pressed against his, and he sampled what she offered, licked the seam of her mouth until she opened. He took over, licking his way around the damp cavern, mimicking what he wished he could do with his body. Pasquale sucked on her tongue, swallowing her moan.

She was a fire in his blood, driving him to want more, need her closer. Pasquale lifted her off her feet, and her legs wrapped around him in response. They didn't have time, Dominic was calling them, but he'd make it for them. Give her something for the gift she gave him.

His Alpha power snaked out, pushing against her skin. Giuliana moaned once more, turning her head until their mouths fit better together. His power danced between her legs, going for fast and hard, tracing what he knew were slick folds ready for his attentions.

Each roll of her hips was a dream. Her cries, a balm to his soul. He wrung her out, dancing on the edge of ignoring the man they both should answer to until she was bucking on him, screaming her climax into the air.

"Delicious," he murmured against her mouth.

"That was … It was only supposed to be a kiss."

"And it was, you just didn't specify which set of lips I was held to."

She slapped his shoulder as he set her on her feet. "We've got to go, dude."

He blinked, not thinking he'd ever been called "dude" before. "Dude?"

"Shut up and let's go."

She was out of his house before he could say anything else. He followed, calling to his wolves who weren't traveling with him to protect Fabiana and the home. Those who would go with him slipped from the night, surrounding him in silence.

Dude?

Shut up, Pasquale!

Make me.

Ugh.

He chuckled, and as one, the group moved, he and Giuliana at the center. She was the only female in the bunch, not because there weren't other strong women in the Bianchi, but because Red couldn't stomach them too close to Pasquale. She was still in mating heat, pushing them to mark each other permanently. They'd been in bed every night, denying themselves to keep from risking an accidental bite that would go too deep, and the wolf was not happy about it.

They slipped from the Bianchi area and onto the main street sloping toward Dominic's home. Other wolves in human form passed them in cars. Since the moment Giuliana knew Pasquale couldn't travel like that, she didn't either. It took longer for them to reach the central area, and by the time they did, men and women were lined in front of the Alpha's house.

Some were clad from head to toe in weapons, glittering guns and knives. Others were in their lupine form, ready to rend and tear with their claws. Pasquale's wolves followed Giuliana and him to the front of the pack before standing at the door to let them continue.

They would protect their Alpha and his mate—from Lombardi wolves if necessary.

He saw the statement and was humbled by it, even if he worried they may trigger the others with their show of force. But no one was concerned about them, and Dominic swung open his front doors.

"In here, now."

Pasquale growled a warning at Dominic's biting tone directed at Giuliana but followed him inside.

I am his Enforcer, mate. Cool it.

When he learns to speak to you properly, I will.

Then forget the wolf part. He's our Capo di tutti Capi. He has earned the right under the Code to speak to me like that.

Fine.

Giuliana's feminine chuckle filled his head and warmed him. She'd become more accustomed to speaking with him and allowing their relationship to flow. He couldn't say that didn't make him happy.

"Silva has healed," Dominic said.

Romano stood next to Silva. He looked like shit. His eyes were bloodshot, his hair stood on end, and the rumpled slacks he wore with his shirt and tie looked like it'd seen better days. He could barely contain the wounded and angry growls leaking from him constantly.

I would be no better if Giuliana were taken.

"The Boulder Alpha gave some information on the Renegades, confirming what you told me, Pasquale. The leader is Alexi Borgia, and he's one of the most powerful shifters they've seen in a long time. And he's also old. Old Country and older wolf."

"Meaning he ties to the old ways," Giuliana surmised.

Dominic nodded, sliding his hands into his pockets. "He is originally from the Ukraine and identifies as a Cossack. His men who follow him are, too, and are some of the most highly trained combatants in the world."

"It won't matter. I'll kill them all," Romano vowed.

"And I will help. But we get Kalinda out first. The letter this Kieran left, and his demands since, are all for Silva to come alone and meet him. But he has realized he's caused an incident by taking a wolf mate."

Romano rolled his shoulder. "If I feed him his dick, he'll remember."

"We will, brother. Silva has agreed to meet his demand, but we won't let her go alone. Her team will be Pasquale, Giuliana, the wolves from the Bianchi, and Zahara, in case anyone needs healing. The rest will come with Romano and me so we can ambush them if anything goes wrong. Romano won't focus on doing anything but getting his mate, and we will give him the opportunity to do so."

The wolves nodded in agreement as Zahara slammed through the front door. "I'm here. The path has been warded as much as I can, directly through to Scorched Earth. I contacted Amalia, and she's also had it cleared, so we have no interference heading into the area from officials. It seems your mate has them scared shitless," she added to Romano.

The large wolf smiled a vicious smile. "As they should be."

"We've got everything in order."

Dominic unfurled his Alpha call, and it raced out, spreading over the land. Pasquale stood tall against it. His own Alpha skill kept him protected from feeling the sting, but Giuliana grunted. Without being mated to him, she wasn't protected by Pasquale's power. He pulled his mate closer to him and helped her stay on her feet.

She would kneel to no man.

"Let's move. I want that location fucking surrounded, like, yesterday. I will remain with Zoey for protection. Don't fuck this up."

At Dominic's order, everyone moved at once. Silva streaked out the door and into the sky, hovering as Pasquale readied on the balls of his feet.

"We can't run all the way there. We'll never make it."

Giuliana's words stopped him short. He didn't want to get into a fucking car. He could outdistance any one of them, but … he knew she wouldn't be able to maintain for that length of time. He cursed under his breath.

"Just ride with me and stay in wolf form."

He couldn't. As a wolf, it would be much easier for his Alpha side to show up now that he'd acknowledged Giuliana as his mate. He shook his head. "I can't risk it."

"Get your ass in the car. It's an order."

He lifted a brow at her, and she blushed but held her ground. "You'll pay for that … later."

He whispered the dark promise in her ear and smiled at her delicate tremble. Yes, his mate loved how he took control.

"For now, let's just get to Kalinda. We can even take some revenge for Heath while we're at it."

She'd changed the subject, but he let it go. He knew finding a way to keep the promise she'd made to Lorenzo meant a lot to her. He'd do everything he could to help her, including get inside a fucking car.

She headed to hers, and he flowed behind her as everyone spread out.

"You don't seem to be any wolf, little boy."

Pasquale jerked to a stop next to Giuliana's car. Zahara was there, almost like she'd appeared out of thin air. Silva still hovered over them, prepared to fly the whole way there.

"Come down into the car, Fae Queen. Conserve your strength."

The Fae alighted right next to Pasquale. No one, not even Silva, argued with Zahara. They piled in, Silva in front next to Giuliana and Zahara in the back.

"I'll help with the fear," she whispered.

How she knew, how she read it in him, he didn't know. But he was thankful she didn't blast it to the whole of the wolves behind him. He forced himself to get into the car next to the witch doctor and let the door close before he shifted into his wolf form.

It didn't matter. His lungs squeezed, and he struggled to suck in a breath.

"Focus on your mate, her scent," the witch doctor told him.

Silva turned around and stared at him. "What's his problem?"

"Nothing," Giuliana and Zahara replied in unison.

Silva's eyebrows disappeared in her hair line. "Okaaaaay."

"It's a state of mind, and you can't be trapped by that. Focus on what will help you."

I'm working on it.

But of course, the witch doctor couldn't hear him.

"Do you know why you're afraid of the Renegades, Giuliana?"

Zahara's sudden change of tactics rendered everyone in the car silent. Pasquale didn't give a shit about his fear anymore. Giuliana's permeated the car, sending Snow into overdrive.

Protect her. She's afraid.

There is nothing here.

Protect her!

Pasquale growled at the witch doctor.

"What do you know about my past?"

"I know there was a woman, hair as red as fire. She protected her daughter … so small … the only thing she had left from a mating with a man long gone."

The car pitched to the side, but Giuliana got it back under control. They flashed forward, her foot heavy on the gas.

"They killed my mother. The Renegades."

The redheaded woman Giuliana spoke of.

Are you sure it was your mother?

I remember.

Fuck. This changed things … just a bit. But the witch doctor had succeeded in something. Pasquale was no longer afraid of the car. He was too focused on his mate and her flying emotions.

Stop the woman from speaking.

She's trying to help, Snow.

Snow's aggravated growl filled Pasquale's head, but he said nothing more.

"Why didn't you say anything before?" Giuliana forced out between clenched teeth.

"I didn't know the woman myself. And I only just picked it up from your man here."

Pasquale sat back on his haunches.

"You are wondering how?"

No, of course not.

He rolled his eyes, and Zahara laughed. "Because I'm me. I healed most of ya, yeah? I been around long enough to tap into the unknown tings. I got the impression, if not the whole."

"What else do you know?"

Zahara shook her head. "Nothing more than that, chile. The woman was never heard of again, and I was … blocked from interacting much with the wolves after that."

Pasquale remembered that before she'd been able to openly claim Dominic as her grandson—something hard to fathom when she looked so incredibly young—she'd had to hide it because of a spell she'd put on him to protect the two of them.

"But now your wolf isn't afraid in the car anymore, and we've got a battle to face. Sort of pisses you off a bit more to know the Renegades have something only they can answer for you, doesn't it?"

There was something deadly about Zahara. Her hazel eyes glittered with rage, and her smile was sharp. She'd shared the info because she'd wanted them prepared for war. She wanted them to join the ranks of vengeance with Romano and Dominic.

Pasquale had already been ready, for Heath alone. Now he had more reason.

Kieran had bitten off much more than he could chew.

CHAPTER FIFTEEN

They reached the Scorched Earth entrance en masse.

They may have been chomping at the bit to get inside, but politics still ruled. A Level-7 mage scanned the occupants of the cars with a neutral gaze, his face shadowed by the black hooded coat he wore. Glowing red runes lit up the skin of his hands as they danced around his fingers in a caressing weave.

Guardian.

Giuliana had only heard of the great mages stationed at Scorched Earth prepared to kill any trespassers. They protected the portal cities from threats. Curious humans may be allowed in so far as to see the edges of the city—where the pretty homes and sparkling paranorms lived—to make them believe there wasn't blood and war within. But if they caused any sort of commotion, they'd never be allowed to return home.

They'd been charged with their duty after the dragon had come into Encantado, blazing a trail of devastation. The runes on their skin locked them to their oath, keeping them on the edge of the city, always separate and yet needed.

"Where is your Alpha?"

Giuliana couldn't help the tremble that spread over her at the mage's voice. It was deep, thick with power.

"I am here."

Dominic stepped forward, his head held high. As an Alpha, he had to show no submission to any below the Council level, and even then, he chose when he did. Kalinda was the only one to get his respect in such a way, but he only did it in official situations.

Otherwise, Romano would never let him hear the end of it.

The mage lifted his hand toward Dominic, and Giuliana crouched, ready to battle.

"Be calm, Enforcer. I am simply checking his reason for being here."

"You could ask," Romano offered, stepping up beside his Alpha. "People lie."

The mage's gaze went white. It was so bright, Giuliana struggled to keep her eyes open as the runes on his hand sped over his skin with dizzying speed.

"*Show me.*"

Loud, so fucking loud. The words were a mark of demand, and Dominic's eyes closed. After a moment, the mage gasped.

"I am Torin. As the Ales is in trouble, you will be allowed entry. I will escort you within Scorched Earth to your destination. Where is the Fae?"

Silva stepped forward, her wings midnight darkness and glittering stars. She wore her Fae armor, this time in all black to match her wings. It was stark against her white hair and violet eyes.

"I am Niamh Danaan of the Silver, and this pack is of my House."

Torin's eyes widened at that, and he glanced at Dominic. "Do you accept?"

For a moment, Giuliana's Alpha's gaze met Silva's. She nodded, and he shrugged. "I accept."

"As pack of the Ales and House of the Fae Queen of Seraph, you will be given immunity to any damages you cause within the Scorched Earth boundary. But let that destruction leak out, and I will end you all."

As threats went, it was pretty badass. Giuliana could feel the weight of it settling around her shoulders, a promise instead of boast.

Who the hell is this Guardian?

Ancient, Red whispered.

How old?

I don't know. Old enough to obliterate you, at least.
Gee, thanks, Red. Aren't you sweet?
You asked.

Giuliana rolled her eyes at her wolf and watched as Dominic waived them forward. "I will head back to my mate. Keep me updated on the status of the battle, do you understand me?"

"Yes, sir!" the wolves called at once.

Pasquale rolled his shoulders, a warrior ready for war. Giuliana appreciated the long lines of his back and his direct stare at Torin.

Alpha.

Torin, as if summoned by her internal thought, surveyed Pasquale for a moment before he turned back toward what looked like a solid wall riddled with names.

Those who died.

It was a memorial to the mages, humans, and other paranorms who'd lost their lives when the dragon came. Torin lifted his hands and placed them on the wall. It shimmered before wavering and disappearing.

The blackened and twisted lands of Scorched Earth spread before them. The ground was cracked and split, some areas still red with undying fire. It seemed to breathe, burping steam and fire in spots.

"The wall keeps the dragon flame from spreading," Torin explained.

"It still burns?" Giuliana couldn't believe it. The dragon had come and gone decades ago; the fire shouldn't be still going.

"To this day. Watch your step and follow closely. The place in your Alpha's mind was once a sacred space."

Giuliana lifted an eyebrow but did as the Guardian said. Pasquale moved first, right on Torin's heels, Giuliana behind him, Zahara next, and his wolves spreading out around them in a tight circle. Romano noticed it, smirking, but said nothing.

The small army kept a tight file, traversing the scorched landscape with sure feet. As wolves, they could sense the ground. Not in the same way as mages, but they knew where it was safe to step and where it wasn't. It worked for them now.

Torin picked up speed, his legs eating up the distance in a hard race, one to rival an ordinary wolf. That was surprising.

Mages, no matter how strong, couldn't move as fast or have the senses a shifter had.

The Guardian was full of surprises.

He cut to the left, and the shifters followed. Silva stayed in the air, barely hovering above the ground. She must have been conserving her strength for the upcoming clash that was sure to happen. As her hair shifted in the breeze, a silver hilt of a sword appeared between her shoulder blades. The Fae Queen was not coming for a simple rescue mission.

Giuliana could understand her resolve. Kieran had crossed a boundary there was no looking back from. No matter what, he'd die today, and Romano's constant growls added to the atmosphere of retribution filling the air.

Heath. Kalinda. Silva.

They'd all been hurt by Kieran's need to have Silva, for a reason none of them were aware of. But it wouldn't matter when they found him.

A flash to Giuliana's left grabbed her attention, but it moved too fast for her to know what it was.

Did you see that?

See what?

Pasquale tossed a look back at her over his shoulder before scanning the horizon.

Maybe it was nothing.

Your senses are strong. We'll keep a lookout.

She liked how he did that. How he took her thoughts and trusted them. No one had ever trusted her so completely. Her heart felt as light as her feet. Maybe, just maybe, they could do it. Figure out the details and give this a chance.

A forest rose from nothing, shimmering in a haze until it solidified.

"The trees are real, no matter what your mind tries to tell you. Dodge them!"

Torin's command reverberated through the air. That was fucking weird. Her wolf senses didn't pick up a single tree even if she could see them. She would have assumed they were a mirage, but at Torin's call, she shifted to dodge the first one as they entered.

A yelp told her a wolf hadn't listened, too cocky and sure of their nose.

"You will die here if you don't listen to exactly what I say."

They would be sure to. The pack pulled closer together, streaking in and out of the trees. Another flash, this time to Giuliana's right, nearly made her stumble to a stop. There was a wolf, one that wasn't with them. But even as Giuliana lifted her nose to the air to sniff, the wolf was gone, and they weren't downwind of it.

Who the hell is that?

A Renegade may be tracking us.

Just saying the name in her head made her hands shake, but she'd grown stronger, facing her memories slowly each day. It didn't stop her as it had before.

This fucking place is messing with my nose. All I smell is soot and fire. Even these dead trees don't smell of wood.

I keep seeing a wolf.

It is probably a scout. We'll have to deal with it when we get there.

Scout or not, they wouldn't be turning around. They had to get to Kalinda. It had been several weeks since she'd been taken, and they didn't want to trust that Kieran wouldn't hurt her now that he knew Silva was completely healed to fight.

It still confused Giuliana as to why he wanted her healed. It would be easier to take an enemy when they were too weak to fight back. Waiting had a sense of honor she didn't trust Kieran to truly have. Not after killing an innocent man or attacking the Council offices under the guise of a Trinity mage. This thing didn't make sense, and Giuliana couldn't help but believe they were heading into an ambush, one they were forced to.

Torin began to slow down, bringing the wolves to a crawl before they stopped. "Ahead, is the old dais."

"They have one here?" Silva alighted next to Torin. "I didn't think mages maintained those anymore."

"This one was preserved before the creation of Scorched Earth."

"Meaning no one could get here to destroy it."

Giuliana stepped forward. "Want to explain what the dais is?"

"We can do that after I get my mate," Romano interrupted.

"The dais is deadly, Romano. It's better to be prepared," Silva warned.

The normally jovial wolf stood to his full height. "*I'm* deadlier."

"The dais was made as a meeting ground for mages and Fae. It's a place of coming to compromise or ending wars."

"He started this war, and we're going to finish it."

"Agreed, but we have to face the truth. He's stacked the odds in his favor. In the dais—"

"We'll move now."

Giuliana had never seen Romano so disagreeable, but she couldn't fault the wolf. If Pasquale were in danger, she didn't think she'd have been able to wait out the time for Silva to heal. Though, to be fair to Romano, Dominic had made Zahara ward the wolf so he couldn't leave his Alpha's home to make sure he didn't sneak out and become a one-man army.

She understood his need to get to his mate as soon as possible. "We will get to her, Romano. She's still alive."

"I know it. I feel her."

Losing a mate would cripple any shifter, no matter how far apart they may be.

"Torin, can we get to them from here?"

Torin nodded. "We're just steps away. The trees block your view, but once we step on the other side, it'll be clear." He closed his eyes a moment, lifting his hand once again. "Eleven souls on the other side."

"Kieran had four Fae and five wolves with him at the Council when he took Kalinda. That accounts for everyone. Be careful of the Fae warrior's spears. The Unseelie tend to put poison on their blades," Silva explained.

"Noted. *Wolves.*"

Romano may not have been an Alpha, but he was a *Capo*, a powerful one. All the wolves with them snarled. Some stayed in their human forms, palming their guns in preparation, others—the Bianchi in particular—shifted into their four-legged other halves. Giuliana allowed herself to partially shift, her fingers tipping with claws and her teeth sharp. If she needed to grab Kalinda and run, she'd make sure she did.

Zahara readied for battle as well, her eyes filling with storms and her hair whipping around her in a blast of air. The white lines and dots on her face were vibrant as her skin darkened. It was … eerie, to see her shift so. The witch doctor, in all her glory.

Torin watched it all before nodding. "You're ready."

He slashed his hand to the side, and the trees parted, bending under his gift to expose the dais. It was a large, flat stone circle with larger rocks standing up around it. Sort of like the human Stonehenge. In the center stood who Giuliana assumed was Kieran, given his triumphant smile and Silva's hiss. Behind him, a golden orb hovered with Kalinda floating within it.

"Romano!"

"Mate!"

Giuliana dared to grip Romano's bulging bicep, keeping him in place. When his gaze ripped to her, she nodded at the warriors around the bubble and the wolves at the ready.

Romano snarled but stayed put.

"I smell Heath."

They all froze at Pasquale's words. Romano recovered first. "What?"

"Heath's scent is all around here. Giuliana, come."

Giuliana stepped forward, already knowing what he needed. She plastered her back to his front, and his power wrapped around her. For the first time, Pasquale exposed himself, and Romano stepped back.

"What the fuck?"

"Just ... wait a second," Giuliana whispered.

The colors of scent surrounded her again, vibrant black to the wolves, a darker, gritty one spiked green for the Fae, and Kalinda was a bright rainbow. But she also saw something else, something that confused her.

The same corded scent she'd seen around the clearing that represented Heath was around the dais, prickly and shivering in a tight circle. Without thought, she reached out to Zahara and Romano. The wolf and witch doctor sucked in a breath.

"What is this?"

"Scent, Romano. As Pasquale sees it."

Romano growled. "Heath ... how is he—"

Kieran stepped forward. "Well met, Niamh. I have one demand, that is all."

"What did you do to Heath? Do you think we'd let you go after you killed him and took my mate?"

Kieran sighed. "I wasn't talking to you, dog. And as for your mate, she's perfectly fine. Silva needed some … encouragement, and I ensured she got it. I gave her time to heal, doesn't that count for something?"

Romano stepped forward, his muzzle flashing to sharp, white teeth. "Commendable enough for me to shorten your death just shy of too much blood and guts."

"You say that as if you could reach me."

Romano lunged forward, and the Fae behind Kieran sprang into action, pressing their spears into the bubble surrounding Kalinda and pointing them at her neck.

"No!" Silva roared.

"I was speaking. It's rude to interrupt. Now, I'll continue. I, Kieran of the Shadow, challenge you, Niamh Danaan of the Silver, to *Osaltirhiem*."

Silva sucked in a deeper breath, breaking away from Giuliana's hold. "All this for a duel?"

"All of this, and a duel to the death. It's time for you to answer for all your crimes."

Giuliana snorted. "Says the Unseelie who killed an innocent man."

Kieran glared at Giuliana before he stepped forward. "I killed no one."

Slowly, Kieran's body shrank, thinning out to a lanky form Giuliana knew so well. Long limbs, black hair just around his ears, the same sarcasm filling his eyes. No longer were his ears pointed, and he had similar height, but none of the impression of a man.

No, he was a teenager with just the promise of what will be.

The scent tracer locked, straightening out, and Giuliana knew exactly who she was looking at before Pasquale said a word.

"Heath."

"This is awkward."

It was the same boyish voice. The sardonic twist to his lips. *Heath*.

"Stop playing games. We know how well you mimic, you fucking bastard," Romano argued.

Kieran pulled a slender phone out of his pocket and dialed. Romano's phone rang, and the wolf growled.

"Can't mimic knowledge. Tell them, Silva."

The Fae, pale and disbelief written all over her features, nodded. "Fae glamour only works on appearance. He wouldn't have known what Heath knew."

"He has his phone. That's easy to figure out," Romano argued.

"Your favorite gun is the Beretta you keep under your pillow. You pointed it at me one time when Dominic made me come get you to teach me a lesson," Kieran said to Romano.

Romano tensed and growled, long and deep. "We came not only for Kalinda but to avenge *you*."

For a moment, Kieran looked sad. "I know. I thought … Silva would come looking for me. But she didn't."

The night Giuliana and Pasquale found the clearing, the trap had been set to confuse a scenter and force them to use a stronger person to map. Maybe even mages to search, and that would have meant Kalinda and Silva.

"You didn't expect Pasquale."

Kieran turned his attention to Giuliana and Pasquale standing together. "I don't think anyone would have planned for him." He looked back to Romano. "I didn't hurt her, like I promised, because of who you all were to me. Give me Silva, and Kalinda is free."

"You know better than to ask for that."

Kieran nodded. "Yes. I see that now. The *Osaltirhiem* is the only way. Step into the circle, Silva, and Kalinda goes free. I swear on my blood."

"Like we'd believe you!"

Putting a staying hand on Romano's arm, Silva stepped forward. "As a Fae, he's bound to the rules of the Blood Duel. Swear to free Kalinda and leave the others unharmed, and I will accept."

"I swear it."

The rune-filled circle on the stone floor of the arena glowed brightly.

"Kalinda will kill me if you die," Romano argued.

"Damn right," Kalinda added.

"It's a good thing I won't die then, isn't it?"

CHAPTER Sixteen

Silva stepped over the binding runes, and the magic in the ancient runes slapped around her. No getting out, no retreat. But for Kalinda, she'd do anything. The minute she was in the circle, the golden holding orb around Kalinda faded, dropping the Ales to her feet.

Crazy woman she was, Kalinda ran right at the circle. "You get out here right now!"

It wouldn't work. "Don't touch the circle."

"Screw you."

Silva wouldn't reach her in time. Kieran blocked that side of the ring, once more showing his true side and not the glamoured image of Heath. Kalinda slammed into the invisible barrier, and sparks rained down as she screamed.

"Kalinda!"

Romano's roar was a call to battle as he leapt into motion. He raced to his mate's side, Pasquale and Giuliana right there with him. The Fae readied their spears, prepared to battle. A bullet whizzed right by Romano's head and slammed into a Fae's chest.

The Unseelie grunted, exposing his fangs, but stayed on his feet.

"Stop it! They won't attack unless we attack. They're here to make sure I fight. Take Kalinda and leave," Silva cried.

"I'm not going anywhere."

Kalinda, standing now, was pale but didn't budge. Romano reached her and dragged her into his arms. She accepted his hungry kiss. "I can't leave her."

"We won't."

Silva's pack, accepted in her House, slipped back to the other side of the circle where Silva stood, and didn't move an inch more. Torin stood to the side, watching it all. As a Guardian, he may have gotten them there, but it wasn't his job to be part of the battle unless they threatened Encantado.

Silva turned her attention to Kieran instead. "They loved you."

"What do you know of love?"

"Why are you doing this?"

"You act as if you don't know, *Queen*." He said her title like a curse. "All you ever did was sit on your throne and let others die."

She'd never been proud of her ruling years. She'd been too young, too confident in her power, just as she was when Kalinda was taken. She hadn't learned from her past, but she hadn't allowed her people to die needlessly.

"The Unseelie court held their own in Daemon. I had nothing to do with their lands from Seraph. You know this."

"And what of the Unseelie trapped in Seraph?"

Unseelie in Seraph? It was impossible. They only mixed under strict guidelines of trade. The two Fae had never gotten along. The Seelie wanted to help humans, giving them magic and assistance. The Unseelie, however, had given them daywalkers and other paranorms that could feed on fragile human life. In retaliation, the sides had separated.

"There were no Unseelie in Seraph."

Instead of answering, Kieran bellowed and leapt into the air. Silva matched him, snapping her wings open to lift into the air. They twisted, spinning and breaking apart. Kieran wasn't able to fly like Silva, but he had power in his legs. The circle would keep her from only being able to fly so high, where he could also reach.

The *Osaltirhiem* kept battlers on even ground, forcing them to meet on terms either could win. It was the reason the Fae had designed it. Knowing this and being locked within the confines were two very different things.

Silva streaked forward, pulling her magic around her to turn her into liquid silver, strong and malleable. Kieran retaliated, wrapping fire around the sword he pulled from his back.

"I'll cleave your head from your fucking shoulders."

He'd try, he meant.

Silva grabbed her sword, infusing it with her power. The silver beast was made up of what she had control over, and the inset diamonds on the hilt amplified her gift. She elongated the blade until it fell apart in shards along a whip.

Keep him distant.

Flicking her wrist, her blade slithered, slicing through the air with a whistle, and wrapped around Kieran. He was fast, though, shifting into shadow and back in an instant to disentangle himself before advancing on her.

She met each step he made with a twist of her weapon, keeping him inching instead of barreling into her. This wouldn't last long. He knew her weakness, what element could be used to cut her to size.

"Are you afraid, little queen? Afraid to face the truth?"

"I fear no one."

"Your name terrifies my people, but not me. I'll avenge them all."

"I did nothing to your people."

"You kept us in chains!"

Kieran leapt into the air, high above Silva's head, turning so he flipped, angling his sword downward. The move was agile, graceful—deadly. As he fell, he blew his fire out behind him, which pushed him faster. She rolled, tucking her chin just as his sword sank into the rock where she'd been standing with a great *boom.*

"We were enslaved. Beaten for sport. Our women taken for enjoyment. We were nothing but playthings for your people. The rich. The powerful. They loved breaking our bones. They loved how we begged to return home. But the shackles they placed on us made us untouchable."

She had no idea of the atrocities of which he spoke. She'd never enslaved the Unseelie. "Never!"

He dragged his armor from around his neck, exposing a thick, black band with white runes pressed into it. She read them, and her soul went cold.

Sorlisalvalkeld.

They'd spelled it out, letter by letter, to etch more pain into the flesh of those bound to them. She recognized it but didn't want to believe it. He'd been a slave. The haunted, vile look in his eyes was pure hatred for her kind. His oppressors.

"I-I didn't do that."

"We cried for you, the great Queen of the Seelie. We cried and begged like our people had never done before. For your kind to have mercy, for you to free us. Instead, you ordered us *killed* for having bothered you."

No! But she couldn't answer him. Couldn't move fast enough as he flashed to her side.

"And all we wanted was our freedom. All we wanted was to *live*."

His fiery blade cut toward her face, and she sprang away. Too slow. Too slow. An inferno spread across her nose where the fire touched, spreading under her eyes and making them water. Silva blinked against the tears, forcing herself to stay on her feet and fight.

But Kieran had rage and pain behind him. She was fighting for her life, but he battled for those who'd lost theirs. Faceless souls she knew nothing about.

"Don't punish me for another's crime."

"It was your seal!"

No one in the Light Palace had access to her seal. It was from her magic, straight from her soul. It kept others from being able to use her name on decrees. She'd never signed an order like that. Had she?

She combed her fractured past for the answer, and all she could remember was her blind acquiescence to whatever was put in front of her. Seraph was rich, it was growing, and the people loved her. Had one of the protocols she'd signed sealed the fate of the Unseelie held illegally in her lands?

"I didn't know."

"You were ignorant to the filth within your own walls. You didn't *care* enough to lead. It's why even Asherah was lost to you."

At her sister's name, she wailed. Yes, Asherah had disappeared, never to be seen again because she hadn't been paying attention. She hadn't thought to send her sister with escort when she wanted to travel to their family homelands. Who would harm her? And Asherah was nothing but a whisper of remembered laughter in the Palace long before Silva even realized she was gone.

Silva had been a horrible queen, distracted and only interested in her life and fun.

And now she would fall. Kieran was too close, his blade already poised at her breast before she could fend him off.

"I never meant it. I swear on my blood."

The blade pierced, and Kalinda screamed.

I'm sorry.

Her heart shattered, the world fading to darkness.

I'm so sorry.

"I never would … have allowed it. I was … not a good queen. I'm … sorry."

The blade stopped, but it didn't matter.

Agony blew through her limbs before giving way to seeping cold.

Kalinda.

The numbness spread through her fingers, up her arms.

The tie!

But the thought came too late. Just like Silva had always been. Too late. Too absorbed.

Never meant to be queen.

She never should have been.

With a final blast of the power remaining inside her, she shot all her silver out of her body in thick spikes. It was automatic, a final plea to live. Each one pierced Kieran as he held on to her, his blackened blood spilling down over her.

Even that couldn't warm her.

"Do you swear it?"

What? She couldn't focus on the words. They filtered in and out of her brain as she coughed, blood choking her.

"Do you swear you knew nothing of it?"

Blood sprayed from her mouth. "I swear it."

Silva stretched. She was so tired. Her fingers were slick, clumsy messes, but she still reached to place them on Kieran's neck.

"I release you, Kieran of the Shadow. No … Heath. Heath, you are free."

The brand sizzled, breaking apart into ashes and flying to the sky. Kieran watched her with wide eyes.

He ripped his blade from her heart, tossing it away. It clattered somewhere, the sound echoing in her head.

Kieran pulled Silva tighter, gripping her against his chest. "Stay, Niamh. Silva!"

But she couldn't, no matter how much she tried.

"Silva!" *Kalinda?*

The magic in the runes snapped again. Kalinda had tried to break in. But until Silva's heart stopped, they couldn't get out, and her spikes hadn't hurt Kieran enough. Even now, the silver cried, molten mercury melting from his body from his inherent heat. He was healing as she lay dying.

"Kalinda!"

Romano's scream made Silva twitch, fight to stay awake, but she couldn't move.

Silva swallowed, forcing her throat to work. "I am her *Cosantiór*. She will …"

"I will get them to safety," Kieran promised.

That's all she could ask.

Kieran shifted, still holding her against his chest, cradling her head on his shoulder. "If you don't get Kalinda to someone, and fast, she will die."

"Not before I kill you first, you piece of shit," Romano roared.

"Silva is her *Cosantiór*," Kieran tried again.

"Explain."

Zahara.

"When Silva's heart stops—" Kalinda wailed, breaking Kieran's words. "Kalinda will die as well. They are tied by the soul. I … didn't know."

No, he hadn't. Heath had disappeared shortly after Silva had come into her Fae powers. He'd run when he sensed her.

When he sensed the one who had abused him and his people may remember and be able to recognize him.

She wanted to hold him close. He may have ended her life, but she couldn't help but understand. What would she have done? If she'd been faced with the same fear, the same hatred, she may have done exactly as he had. She couldn't hate him for wanting to pick up his sword.

And with her memories still jumbled, Silva couldn't remember why she'd been bound and thrown into the world in the first place. Maybe ... maybe it was because of what she'd done to them.

"Run," she whispered.

"What?"

"They'll never let you go. Find a way ... some way, to get home."

"I ..."

"Run, Heath."

Kieran lowered her to the ground, his eyes filled with silvery tears. "I'm sorry."

But then he was gone, moving as fast as his wounds would let him get to the edge of the circle. He wouldn't be released until she was gone, but he could prepare.

"Bring a portal!"

"You're not getting away, you fucking bastard."

"Silva!"

The voices were so loud, and she couldn't tell who was screaming as it all happened at once. Silva forced her head to turn and find Kalinda. Her girl was just steps away on the other side of the circle. She cried on her knees, reaching as close to the circle as she dared.

"I love you, chocolate drop."

Kalinda's watery chuckle warmed Silva's fading heart.

"I love you too. I heard ... what he said."

"Let him go, Kalinda." Silva didn't hear the response. She was too tired. "I'm sorry I'm going to see you on the other side so soon."

Because for one to die, the other would too. And that's what Silva regretted more than anything. Kalinda would suffer because of Silva's mistake.

Asherah, I won't be able to keep my promise.

Giuliana grabbed Kalinda and yanked her to her feet just as the circle's power faded and Silva stared at them with sightless eyes. Kalinda wailed, her body bowing like it'd been electrocuted.

"Romano!"

The wolf skidded to a stop in his pursuit of Kieran sliding toward a portal and raced back to Kalinda's side.

"Mate."

Kalinda wasn't listening. She foamed at the mouth, her body jerking back and forth. She had no wounds, but with each passing second, she grew more ashen.

"She's dying. Help her!"

Giuliana was already moving, laying Kalinda on the ground as softly as she could. Pandemonium ensued around them as the wolves fought with the Renegades and the dark Fae who protected Kieran's retreat. But all Giuliana could afford to focus on was the Ales.

Kalinda was unresponsive, and Giuliana spread her hands over Kalinda's chest until they glowed green. She called on every bit of healing power she had. Zahara tossed lightning bolts at the Fae, driving them back and widening the space around Kalinda and Giuliana until there was a buffer of silence.

"Kieran!"

But he was gone, having slipped into a portal. His Fae and the Renegades went with him as well, zapping out of Scorched Earth instantly.

They'd failed to avenge Kalinda … or save Silva.

Zahara raced to Giuliana's side. "Let me see, chile."

Giuliana kept Kalinda in healing stasis but moved over to let Zahara examine her. The witch doctor touched Kalinda everywhere.

"Her soul is fading."

"Then bring it back," Romano cried.

"I'm going to, pup. But not here. This place messes with magic. We need to get to my home. Torin, you have a portal you can create?"

The Guardian shook his head. "Not my gift. At the edge of Scorched Earth, there is one there who can."

"Then we run. It's Kalinda's only hope."

"What about Silva?" Giuliana wasn't leaving her behind.

"Carry her. I'll pack Kalinda," Romano ordered.

Their charges in hand, they raced for a chance to save at least one of their pack members.

CHAPTER SEVENTEEN

The portal deposited Zahara, Silva, Kalinda, Romano, Pasquale, and Giuliana in front of what looked like a log cabin built into a forest. Giuliana had never seen anything like it and knew of nowhere in Encantado like this. Even the Greenwald didn't boast such a beautiful space. Where the hell were they? A massive tree full of deep roots grew through the center of the house and made up the stairs to the main door.

Zahara took the roots faster than lighting. "Stay out here. Lay Silva to the right side of Kalinda on the ground. Make sure their hands are touching. Giuliana, don't stop working on keeping Kalinda here."

They moved, not asking a single question. There wasn't any time to think of anything else. Silva wasn't breathing, and Kalinda was struggling to suck in any air. With each passing minute, their situation got worse. Still, Giuliana was surprised Zahara wanted Silva to be part of the healing process for Kalinda. How could the dead assist?

Romano cleared an area and laid his mate on the soft grass before Giuliana lowered Silva next to her. Giuliana didn't want to focus on how cold Silva was. She knew the circle would have only been broken by her death, but she didn't want to imagine the Fae gone. Everyone groaned when Silva showed up with her spell phone in hand, ready to take the craziest pictures, but they all loved her. There was no doubt of that.

She'd been too vibrant, too full of life.

And everyone had heard Kieran's accusations against her and her responses. Romano would never stop hating Kieran—Heath—after he'd harmed Kalinda by taking Silva's life, but Giuliana couldn't ignore the pain in his voice.

Could any of them say they'd do anything differently?

Giuliana pushed away thoughts of Kieran and stationed herself at Kalinda's head. The Ales was fading quickly, her body cool to the touch. But Giuliana only focused on holding her heart here. She'd never used her gift to this level. For her, healing was reknitting the skin, veins, and bones back together from the inside out, holding that picture in her mind. But with Kalinda, there was no wound to put back together.

What the hell was she supposed to do?

She pushed harder, reaching deep into her reserves to anchor Kalinda's soul to her body. It wanted to escape, to travel with Silva. Giuliana now had a deeper understanding of what it meant for Silva to be Kalinda's *Cosantiór*. To be soul-tied like that was similar to mating between shifters.

Like mates.

"Pasquale!"

He was at her side instantly. "What do you need?"

"Do you think you can do that thing with me for my healing like you do with your scenting ability?"

He frowned. "I don't know, but we'll try."

He surrounded her, putting his arms next to her and intertwining their fingers. The green light from her healing wrapped around his hands lovingly. After a moment, it spread up their arms, and he inhaled deeply next to her ear.

The world brightened, impossible so, colors so vibrant they hurt. The leaves on the trees weren't just green. They were all over the palette of mixes—gold, orange, red, and even blue. Each pulsed with *life*.

The tones bled into the air, twisting and turning much like scent did, but Giuliana saw it differently. It was the life of the earth, right there for her to use. She sank against Pasquale, pulling on his power more.

Take what you need, Giuliana.

Snow. He was there too, hovering over Red. She had her nose to the air, breathing deeply, and pulling from the air.

Like this, Giuliana. Take it.

Giuliana mirrored her wolf, lifting her face into the wind and breathing deeply. Pure essence filled her lungs, and she gathered it in her chest before leaning down and breathing it over Kalinda. It pressed into Kalinda, forcing her color back. It wasn't permanent, but it kept her from slipping over the precipice no one could grab her back from.

"Good, chile. More."

She was so focused on her work, she hadn't heard the witch doctor return. Giuliana did as Zahara asked, pulling more from the world around her to give to Kalinda. Her head was swirling, but she fought to contain the energy.

"Romano, hold your mate's other hand. Let her know what to come back to."

Giuliana didn't pay attention to him, concentrating on giving Kalinda what she could.

"I'm going to use Silva's blood. Giuliana, whatever happens, don't you let her go."

"Yes, ma'am."

Zahara pulled out a wicked blade and sliced open Silva's palm. Putting her hand back with Kalinda's, she lowered them to the ground. She then stepped back, her white gown fluttering on the wind. Zahara had changed and her face was all white along with a white headwrap on her head.

She danced, singing a song Giuliana couldn't understand. Faster and faster she moved, swaying back and forth with her dress flying out around her. Drums filled the air from somewhere unknown and matched her rhythm. They moved as partners.

"*Omi tutu. Ona tutu. Ile tutu. Ori tutu. Tutu Esu. Tutu Orisa. Tutu Egun mi. Tutu bobo Egun ara orun tiembelese Oludumare.*"

Zahara kept going, lifting her head to the sky as she sang. Giuliana poured more magic into Kalinda. Zahara moved closer to the prone women, pushing her hands at them.

"Hear me!"

The ground vibrated underneath them, but Zahara didn't hesitate. She danced with the earth's vibrations. Lightning shot through the sky.

"*Kawo Shango. Modupe Ogun.* Come to me, for I am the Mother of Nine."

The lightning danced, streaking down and shattering around Zahara. The trees seemed to lean to meet her, the earth rising under her feet. Rain pelted their bodies, a pure torrential storm created with Zahara at the center.

She laughed, a sound that wasn't her own. Her eyes hazed with purple, and machetes slipped from her skirt. Nine in all, they danced around her, glinting in the lightning and dancing as thunder boomed.

Silva and Kalinda lifted into the air and hovered at eye level with Giuliana. Zahara directed the storm at Silva. The Fae twitched and jerked. Blast after blast of lightning struck her heart with a forceful punch.

"Ogun, former of the body, knit her back together. Shango, give life to her heart. Obatala, bring back her consciousness!"

Zahara was screaming now, her words almost manic as she moved. She continued chanting, stomping her feet in groups of threes as she moved. Finally, one of the blades shot away and Giuliana heard a deer wail. Another blade whizzed by, and each of them were met with a cry.

Blood. Offering.

Giuliana didn't know why those words entered her mind. But the earth's life increased, pushing more inside her with every inhale.

Take what you need as you asked, daughter.

More power fed into Giuliana, and she fed it into the maelstrom, enraptured by Zahara's connection with the very elements and their acceptance of Giuliana as well.

Silva grunted. Fucking grunted!

Kalinda moaned.

"Mate!"

"Silva."

Zahara fell to her knees, palms still raised toward Kalinda and Silva. She held one, even as the lightning shocked right next to her and the earth jerked hard enough to send them all to their asses. Zahara anchored it all, worked with it, and was one.

The storm faded, leaving behind a refreshing spray of a summer shower, the sun peeking out through the trees. It was deafening, the sudden silence when there had been so *much* before. But in the quiet, Giuliana picked out a beautiful sound.

Breathing.

Silva inhaled, her chest rising, and when she exhaled, Kalinda drew a breath. The worked in tandem, each slowly opening their eyes as one.

"Where … where am I?"

Cheers met Silva's hesitant question. Never in a million years did Giuliana think Zahara would be able to save both of them. Silva sat up gingerly, and Giuliana pulled the Fae into her arms.

"You scared me to death, Tinker."

"My head hurts too bad to punch you for that, so I'll do it later. Ugh." Silva gasped. "Kalinda."

"I'm here. *Oof.* Romano, I can't breathe."

"You can talk, you can breathe, mate."

"Okay. I can't breathe *well*."

"I thought I'd lost you."

Kalinda wrapped her arms around her mate, pulling him close. "I'm here."

They trembled, clutching to one another. Giuliana swallowed against emotions clogging her throat. They'd almost lost Kalinda and Silva, which would have also lost them Romano. But somehow, Zahara had saved them.

"Zahara?"

The witch doctor moaned before she sat up. Giuliana choked. Zahara was changed. Her headwrap fell to the side, leaving her hair wild around her face, but it was gray. Though still beautiful, she was older. There were deep lines on the sides of her mouth and feathers of crow's feet out from the sides of her eyes.

Silva reached for her. "What did you do?"

Zahara only shook her head, gingerly rising to her knees. Her hips popped as she moved. "Just gave up some vitality."

"*Just* gave up some vitality? Are you crazy?"

The witch doctor turned hard eyes on Romano. "I can still kick your ass, pup. Want to try it?"

Even her voice was different, thicker. Giuliana shook her head. "We thank you … but—"

"My great-grandbaby needs her aunt. I wasn't going to let her go."

Kalinda moaned. "Oh, Zahara."

"I've lived for a very long time, Ales. Life eventually catches up. I couldn't save my daughter, but I wasn't going to watch anyone else be taken from Dominic. Not a single person I could help. It is done."

"You can't do that again."

Zahara snorted at Romano. "I can do what I want." She tried to stand, but her legs gave up. "Except stand, it seems."

Romano stood his mate up before he went to Zahara. He lifted her off the ground and hugged her close. "Thank you, Zahara."

"Always. Now I must rest. It's going to take some time to get these energies all the way appeased. Take your mate home and let your Alpha know what has happened."

"Come with us. We can keep an eye on your recovery," Romano returned.

"I need this place. It's close as to possible to untamed land."

Giuliana looked around. "Are we still in Encantado?"

"Yes and no. We are in the Greenwald but in a place you could never reach unless I allowed you."

"You always lived near Dominic," Romano realized.

"Don't tell him. He'll fuss about my moving onto the lands."

"Can you? If you can close off this area, can't you bring it with you into the protected area?"

"I have never thought to try. Perhaps. Hold on."

Zahara closed her eyes and reached her hands up to the sky. Romano held her through it all, seeming to give her whatever he could. He didn't have gifts like Giuliana or Silva, but he'd been able to create something special with Zoey.

"This is going to be wild," Zahara said, laughter echoing her words.

The world swished and swirled, and then righted itself instantly. Giuliana covered her mouth to keep from getting sick. At least they weren't moving anymore. Zahara flicked at a space over Romano's shoulder. It opened and Dominic stood there, shirtless, eyes wide, and Zoey peeking behind them.

"What the fuck are you doing in my bedroom?"

Unfazed, Zahara laughed harder. "I'm home, grandson."

Dominic stared at the older woman in Romano's arms. "*Nonna?*"

"We have a lot to explain, but maybe not in your bedroom, yeah?"

Zahara cackled. "Romano asked me to move in, so I did. I'll have to change the portal location. Wouldn't want to randomly see Dominic's ass in the air."

The group, worn and exhausted from battle and almost losing some, laughed. Zahara stayed true to her word and moved her portal. They entered and were facing away from Dominic's home. Somehow, Zahara's home was in a space *right where Dominic's was.*

"I'll move it later, when I'm less tired. For now, this is as good as I could do. My power just sought him out."

Translation: her love for him was the only thing she had the strength to conjure after what she'd done.

In awe of her power, Giuliana bowed to the Alpha's grandmother but kept silent with her thoughts.

They were home, that's all that mattered. They would live to fight another day.

CHAPTER EIGHTEEN

Pasquale led Giuliana to his home long after all the explanations were made. Dominic released them to rest and ordered they'd make the outcome known to the pack the next day. He'd wait to talk to Lorenzo first, before anyone else, to give him a chance to know what had happened with his friend.

Giuliana still didn't know how to think about Kieran and his life among the pack before he'd revealed who he really was. It was easy to blame him. And maybe if Silva and Kalinda had died, she'd be more inclined to condemn him. But they hadn't, and in reality, neither had Heath. Minor injuries were all that was left after everything went down.

In the outcome, one could say they'd made it out of the war without a scratch.

Of course, Giuliana had seen all they'd faced and knew the truth. They'd nearly been broken, and there were still so many unanswered questions. No matter what, Silva *had* been Queen of the Fae—well, still was—but there were atrocities happening in her name. Going home wasn't an option with Kalinda having to stay in Encantado, her sister was still missing, and they didn't know the story around that.

And Kieran had escaped.

There was no telling what would come in the days ahead. The amount of hell they'd faced in just under a year was terrifying, to say the least.

"Penny for your thoughts?"

Pasquale hesitated in front of his door, the shadow of his porch leaving his eyes glittering in the darkness.

Giuliana sighed. He was still the most incredible man she'd ever lay eyes on. "We've been through a lot."

"The pack, or us?"

"Both. It makes me wonder if there's something larger at work. I know it sounds crazy, but look at Romano and Zoey having the Miracle Grow, the way we can enhance each other's gifts, Kalinda and Silva."

"I'd say we've gotten stronger."

"Maybe, but it makes me think there may be something huge coming. Sort of like the action movies, you know? Heroes show up when there is a greater evil out there."

Pasquale was quiet as he stepped into her space. "Today has taught me one thing, for sure." His hot palm slipped along her jaw, lifting her gaze to his.

"What is that?"

"I watched a man almost lose his mate today, without having said all the things he wished. Without having a chance to see the life they'd live. I don't want to be that man. I'd rather have what we could be than dream of what will never be."

She sucked in a breath, letting him pull her against his hard frame. His fingers danced over her skin, a prayer, memorization. She leaned in, soaking in what she could.

"The first time I saw you, I thought you were the most beautiful creature ever formed. I thought you'd make any man happy to have you. And then I knew you were *mine* to have. And I was afraid, Giuliana. Afraid of what that would mean. Afraid of the cage it would put us both in. I've been terrified all my life because of my father."

Pasquale pulled her closer. "I never knew when he'd call for my death or when he'd realized how much Fabiana meant to me and use her against me. I never knew when he'd force me to fight him, or if I'd win."

"You're stronger than him."

"It's hard, at times, to see that when you're scared of the very thing that could break you. My Alpha power would rip my people apart, and they deserved more."

"And now?"

His lips were close to hers, a breath away and yet so far. She wanted them on her, wanted to feel his touch without caring about what *could* happen.

"And now, mate, I'm not afraid anymore. I *will* have you. I *will* claim you. Because you are worth more than anything I could ever fear, except losing you."

His mouth crashed against hers, sealing her fate. They were a storm, battering each other, pushing and pulling. Pasquale touched her everywhere—groping her breasts, her hips, the curve of her ass—and lifted her against the hardness between his legs.

Mine!

Giuliana didn't even pay attention to which of their wolves cried out. Either way, the answer was a resounding yes. She didn't want to run anymore; she didn't want to escape. Giuliana wanted to be caught by the one man strong enough to make her love the chase as much as the capture.

The one man meant to *truly* be her Alpha.

She wanted him to give her all the things she'd never thought she'd have.

A mate.

Happiness.

Belonging.

With Pasquale by her side, she knew she'd never be ignored again or have anyone put her safety above the idea she had a brain. He'd shown that when he fought by her side to get Silva and Kalinda back. She didn't doubt he would continue to be there for her.

She sucked his full bottom lip into her mouth, moaning her need. He slammed her back against his front door long enough to force it open, and then they were tumbling inside. Fuck getting to his bed. She wanted him here and now.

She bucked, fighting him, knowing he'd answer the challenge.

He didn't disappoint.

He slapped her ass in warning. "Simmer down."

As if.

Her feet pressed into the backs of his knees, sending them tumbling to the floor together. He growled, but she wasn't afraid. He let her fight. He encouraged it. He wanted her to show her strength, and it was freeing. So freeing.

"Needy, Alpha mate."

His words made her tremble. "Yes, *Alpha*."

It was his turn to shake, and power filled his eyes. "Is that what I am?"

"Yes. My Alpha, my mate."

With soft fingers, Pasquale pushed strands of hair behind the delicate shell of her ear. Her heart stuttered in her chest. He was so strong, and his lick of Alpha power only warned of what she knew would come. Giuliana gripped the edge of a stair under her butt and rolled her hips against his cloth-covered cock. She wanted him, wanted everything he could give her.

She wanted to take everything he would give.

Lifting to his knees and angling up her body, Pasquale didn't disappoint. "Let's see, shall we?"

He straddled her chest and pulled his cock from his jeans. Giuliana couldn't look away as Pasquale pressed the tip of his shaft downward and traced her lips. He was soft, velvet smooth, and warm.

"Taste me."

It wasn't a question, even in the quiet way he said it. He worked his hips in a small circle, pressing his cock against her skin. She wanted him, all of him. Slowly, she snaked out her tongue, tasting the tip. He'd get this on her terms, as she wanted.

Pasquale hissed his pleasure, pressing against the flat of her tongue. "More."

Taking her time instead, she opened her mouth and exhaled in a rush, caressing his skin with the heat of her breath. He let her take her inhale before he pressed more of himself inside.

"Good girl."

Just like when he'd claimed her between her legs, he didn't stop there. Pasquale rocked back and forth, and Giuliana used her hot tongue to dance over the tip of his cock. She'd give him warm, wet heat to slip into. He groaned, grinding against her chin as he slid farther inside.

He was thick, broader than any man she'd been with, and her jaw ached from his size, but even that was sexy in this moment. She wouldn't be defeated by his strength. She'd match him in every way.

"Suck."

She closed her lips around him and matched her suction to his strokes to provide a counterbalance. She hadn't taken nearly half of him and it was a struggle to control her breathing comfortably. But she sucked in a deep breath through her nose when he pulled out, and she let him slide back in.

She growled, holding the note so it went down his shaft.

"*Fuck*, that's hot."

She did it again just to prove a point. To drive his need higher. He was being gentle and she wasn't going to be treated like some fragile piece of glass. Giuliana forced her mouth open wider and sucked him deep on his next downstroke.

Pasquale froze, and then tangled his free hand in her heavy mass of hair and kept her head pinned to the step below her. Giuliana bucked underneath him, enjoying the game, thrashing about.

Pasquale took her mouth through it all. He rolled against her textured tongue, slid in the heat, and gave in. His gaze stayed on hers, studying, watching. The minute it appeared she was in real distress, he'd stop. She know it without a doubt, and it let her express her desires the way she wanted to. She had never felt anything this good, this wild. Something more than a quick satisfaction, more than perfunctory motions to get off. She needed him to take her like she needed her next breath.

Giuliana's throat tightened around his head, urging him to take her.

Fuck, yes.

His cry in her head was filthy and uncouth. It was wild and untamed. She'd done that, brought out this animalistic side of him. *She* had that power, no one else. It was heady, knowing that. She grabbed his ass, urging him harder and faster into her mouth. He shifted, lifting a bit higher over her face.

Just like that.

He was rebuilding her, tearing down every pain anyone else had caused. Showing her how strong she was and letting her set the pace. It uplifted her, wrapped her in gossamer and steel. Piece by fucking piece.

Giuliana shifter her tongue in a different way. She sucked hard as he glided into her mouth, so much her cheeks hollowed out. And then she released him as he slid out, turning her head as much as she could.

Yes.

He roared, but she didn't stop sucking him. Didn't stop guzzling him. She wanted him, needed him. Wanted him to explode all over her tongue.

Another night.

When he pulled from her mouth, she cried out in loss.

"I'm here, baby. Right here."

He flipped, a rough turn of his hands, and helped her get on her hands and knees on the stairs. He lifted to his feet, bracing one between her knees.

"Do you want me?"

"Yes," she cried.

"Right here?"

"Take me."

His power leaked out and ripped at their clothing. In seconds they were pressed together, their flesh heated and his cock nuzzled against her ass. He didn't wait, didn't give her a chance to catch her breath. He pulled back, aligned, and slammed home.

She screamed, but he took her higher. Each pointed stab into her made her body clench. His hands on her hips were the only things keeping her from falling forward. Her breasts jiggled with each rough hit, and she wanted him to make her lose her mind.

Somehow, Giuliana gained the strength to lift her upper body, and he helped her. His arm was a thick band over her ribs, and he used his other hand to keep her back arched for his thrusts.

"More. Please more."

Pasquale didn't let her beg much longer. His power washed over her, the same tendrils she felt in her house so long ago. They licked their way over her skin, and she was undone. They played with her nipples and flicked her clit with precision. Pasquale was everywhere, pulling her under a wave of pleasure.

She gasped, barely able to breathe.

I claim you as my mate, from this day and forever more.

His teeth slid into the juncture where her neck met her shoulder. The sting unfurled into agonizing pleasure. They were locked, their magic twirling and meshing as one. Even as he punctured her skin, her healing gift instantly closed the wound. Yet he didn't let go. Over and over he marked her, sending his possession deeper within her.

Her heart pounded, her thighs clenched, and she was nothing more than one long nerve. He plucked her, sending shocks of sweetness pouring over her. Giuliana coated him in liquid eat with each push. Wet sounds echoed in the room as he took her.

Mine.

Mine.

Yours.

Yours.

They claimed each other, pulling and wrapping all the fear of the day into a ball until it fed what they were now doing. She couldn't risk losing him without having known this moment. Without having had him claim her.

Tears sprang to her eyes.

She'd been so alone for so long. Red had walked beside her, but most of the time she thought she was crazy. Dominic had so many pressures with Arturo, and then taking his own pack. Giuliana hadn't been the easy friend with the other women as much as she'd wished.

Until this moment, she hadn't realized how she'd needed something that was *hers*.

Pasquale and Snow belonged to her as much as she did them.

They were their own pack, separate from any others. No matter what happened, she'd have them behind her.

Always.

Pasquale's assurance made her stomach tighten.

He sank a bit behind her, changing the angle, and slammed upward, hitting a spot that made her gasp. He moved faster, taking her roughly. She let him, reveled in him.

She wasn't glass. She wasn't so weak she'd break.

He showed her in his motions that he wouldn't.

As the pleasure spiraled up through her gut, she clung to him. It tightened, bursting apart.

Giuliana Moretti had finally been claimed.

CHAPTER Nineteen

The sun filtered into the bedroom through partially open blue shades, and Giuliana figured she wouldn't be sleeping anymore. The unfortunate thing about her job as Enforcer was, she was used to being up at the crack of dawn to work. Even on days she *really* wanted to sleep in, she didn't seem to get much further than nine a.m. no matter what she did. She peered at the clock beside Pasquale's bed. Well, at least it seemed she'd made it closer to ten.

She could be thankful for that.

Giuliana reached out for her mate and found the other side of the bed empty. She supposed he wasn't exactly one to sleep the day away. Too bad. She was really looking forward to "good morning" sex. It would have been nice.

She stretched, joints popping as they realigned. A dull ache in her shoulder made her smile. Her healing abilities notwithstanding, a mating bite was going to hurt until it healed all the way. She placed her fingers over it, sensing the heat of Pasquale's claim slipping up from it.

She wasn't no longer a single wolf. That was … sort of crazy to even think of. But it was what it was. She sat up slowly, her legs still a bit weak from Pasquale's attentions the night before. She'd have to make sure to be careful when she stood up.

After a moment, she sent out her senses to see who may be around. The wolves she'd begun to recognize as Pasquale's unofficial

Enforcers were hovering around in the front yard, and someone was in the house.

Fabiana.

The scent didn't bother her like it had before. Knowing Fabiana had been a victim as much as Giuliana made her want to get to know her mate's sister. Giuliana got into the shower and dressed, hoping the wolf wouldn't leave. When she was finished, she put on a pair of leggings and willowy peasant top. It felt good to be back in her regular clothing. Without a mission, she didn't have to be so militant.

Giuliana followed her nose to find where Fabiana was in the house.

When she found her, Fabiana was standing in front of an easel with paint all over her fingers in a wide-open room full of bright windows. But that's not what made Giuliana freeze. No. It was the scarred wolf with reddish-black fur taking up most of the picture standing next to an unfinished woman with blazing red hair.

"Why are you painting her?"

Fabiana gasped and spun around, tripping over the drop cloth. Giuliana snapped forward, keeping the painting and its creator from falling to the floor.

Fabiana sucked in a steadying breath. "Thank you."

Giuliana heard her, but up close, the painting had her mesmerized. The fur of the wolf almost looked real, as if it could leap of the canvas in an instant. Giuliana lifted hesitant hands toward it.

"Don't. It isn't dry."

Caught, Giuliana lowered her hands and stepped away from Fabiana. "I'm sorry. She …"

Fabiana frowned. "You know her."

Maybe. "I don't know. I saw a wolf in Scorched Earth when we went to get Kalinda, but things got crazy and I didn't get to find it."

Her eyes were once more drawn to the woman with bright-red hair Even unfinished, she was almost afraid to look away. She knew the gentle swell of that cheek. The way her dark-green eyes snapped with fire. Her hair, odd for their people—

Their people?

"You know her."

Fabiana seemed to speak without questions. By studying people and situations, generally spoke in statements. She cocked her head to the side and locked her gaze on Giuliana.

"I don't know. It's … a memory."

"That's a first. Most of the time when I paint, I get told I'm crazy. Or my father would destroy them."

"Your father was a dick."

Fabiana snorted, and the sound seemed to surprise her. She peered back and forth in the room like someone would punish her for it.

"No one will ever touch you again," Giuliana swore.

Fabiana tucked a thick patch of dark hair behind her ear with a small smile. "You sound like Paz."

"Well, we *are* mates. Doesn't make the statement any less true."

Fabiana searched Giuliana's eyes. "You mean it. Okay. Hold on."

Giuliana waited, wondering what the hell the woman was doing. Fabiana was like a flame flickering in the wind that could go out any minute. After some shuffling and muttered curses, Fabiana came back into the room with several canvases tucked under her arm.

"What do you think of these?"

Giuliana let her set them up but only looked at Fabiana. She was nervous, wringing her fingers in front of her lap.

She's afraid I'll be like everyone else.

Giuliana understood that, probably better than anyone. They were two children raised under an Alpha's thumb. Giuliana, for the first time, could be thankful Arturo had never wanted to physically hurt her unless he wanted to dole out punishment for her escape acts. Though he never actually did it. Fabiana had faced her father wrath so much her spirit had broken.

If Giuliana did the same thing, Fabiana would shut down. Giuliana didn't even know if Fabiana had shown these to her brother.

"You're not crazy, Fabiana."

"Look at them first, and then tell me that."

So Giuliana did what she asked, starting from the first one. It was a painting of a murky world, in shades of black and grays. Even the grass seemed to be shards of broken black glass. But in the center were three women, billowing out of the darkness. The one in the center held a light in her hands and looked like she was attempting to crush it. The woman on her left had her hands stretched toward the light, anger and fear on her face. But the third woman reached out to the viewer, her hand poised to rip through the canvas.

Giuliana felt chills race down her back just seeing it.

She couldn't tell the age or dress of the women; she felt impressions more than anything. They were wrapped in the darkness itself. But the only one she seemed to hate instantly was the one in the center.

What the hell?

Giuliana didn't make her thoughts known aloud. Instead, she looked to the next painting. This one had wolves and people racing toward a great—

"That's in Scorched Earth!"

Giuliana had just been there. Fabiana hadn't drawn all the faces, but Giuliana recognized the golden orb hovering in the back and the lone Fae standing in the center of the circle. No one but the ones who'd gone and Dominic knew what happened in Scorched Earth. Fabiana shouldn't have been able to draw it from this bird's eye view.

"It's real?"

Giuliana ignored Fabiana's question and looked to the next one. This one had a broken Fae, bloodied and with a fire-laced sword screaming at the woman who'd been in the center of the first painting. In one arm he had a woman in light tucked to his side.

Kieran?

No, Fabiana was not crazy, not by any stretch of the imagination.

"Have you shown these to Pasquale?"

Fabiana shook her head. "I see these in dreams, and I can't get them out of my head until I paint them. This last one, the wolf, has been showing up since you came to the house."

The wolf—the one Giuliana had seen in the woods for only a flash. Next to the bright-red woman she could just barely remember.

She dropped to her knees.

"Giuliana?"

"You're not crazy, Fabiana. Never let anyone tell you this. Your brother needs to see this."

"No! He'll destroy them."

Fear permeated the air. Fabiana grabbed her paintings and hugged them to her chest. She was so broken, so tortured because of the hell of her father.

"Fabiana, I will never lie to you. What you painted, two of them I recognize, and I may know a person from another."

Fabiana looked up at her with a fragile hope in her eyes. "He won't take them?"

"Pasquale is not your father. But if he tried, I'd kick his ass for you."

"You're nothing like my father said you were."

Giuliana rolled her eyes. "We've established your father was an ass. But what did he say?"

"That you were cruel, just like your uncle. He said you only cared about having life the way you wanted and you should have been put down."

Giuliana growled. Of course, she'd wanted her own life and to be free of the bullshit she was forced to endure to stay safe. She hadn't wanted to be wrapped in gossamer and steel, protected from so much as a hangnail. She'd wanted to be free to be who she was and live life her way.

But to a man like Primo—because she refused to call that bastard a wolf—she probably was someone he wanted killed.

"Your father had an issue with women who spoke their mind. He didn't like anyone who could challenge him."

Fabiana watched Giuliana for a moment. "My father thought women were only good for breeding." She tilted her chin toward the windows. "Most of the wolves in our pack were males, did you notice?"

"I did, but that is to be expected. Not all have found mates and won't risk having long-term relationships if they know they could meet their intended one day."

Fabiana shook her head. "It's more than that." She closed her eyes. "The women of Bianchi either bred with him and his chosen wolves when asked, or they were put to death."

Giuliana sucked in a breath. "An Alpha has to breed with a mate. He can't just have children outside of that. Otherwise, one could have an army of Alpha-powered males who'd tear the pack apart for control."

Fabiana's gaze was dark, a direct challenge. "Yes."

What the hell had been wrong with Primo? What he'd tried to do was impossible, and the wolves had to know it. Children between mated pairs was easy enough, but unmated pairs tended to be unable to see a pregnancy through to birth. It was a quirk of their species, perhaps, but it was a known fact.

"Why did he do it?"

"So they would fear him. Wolves would fight to be one of the chosen few because they had a chance to mate. Then they had a chance for the women important to them not be taken by others. Without that protection …"

In short, Primo found ways to destroy both the women and men under him until they followed blindly in order to protect themselves.

I'd gut him if he were still alive. Feed him his balls like Hannibal.
Red, you're getting right bloodthirsty, but I'd help you.

"You're talking to your wolf."

"Yes. We're deciding how we would have killed your father if he were still alive."

That elicited a surprised laugh from Fabiana. "How can you be so strong?"

Giuliana stepped up to Fabiana, crowding her space. The younger woman bowed, fear leaking from her. Fabiana tucked her chin, not daring to look Giuliana in the face.

"Look at me," Giuliana ordered.

"I-I can't. You're an Alpha mate."

"And you are the daughter of an Alpha. You are not weak. I don't care who stands before you, you look them in the fucking eye. Right here, Fabiana. Right now, claim who you are."

The woman forced her shoulders back. It was slow, painfully slow, but she lifted her head in degrees. Her fists were clenched at her side, but she raised her face. When Fabiana's gaze met Giuliana's, neither woman said a thing. They looked at each other, two daughters of Alpha blood. Two women who'd been controlled by those around them.

Sisters in the sense of sharing experiences others would not understand.

She is fragile and can shatter like glass, but I am unbreakable.
So I will give her some of my strength.

"I swear to you, I will never let you be hurt again. When you're ready, I will teach you how to defend yourself, I'll help you find your voice. And I've got an idea of how to start."

"O-okay."

Giuliana went to get her phone, dialing even as she rushed back to Fabiana. The dark-haired woman was still standing where she left her when someone answered the call.

"Giuliana? What's wrong?"

"Can you get to Pasquale's house?"

Fabiana lifted a brow, but Giuliana shook her head. She wasn't going to tell her who she'd called just yet.

"Is everything okay?"

"I have a woman here who needs some girl time. One who's been … hurt."

"I'm on my way."

Giuliana hung up the phone, smiling at Fabiana's nervous expression. Giuliana had a feeling. She knew just who could help get Fabiana facing power and still be comfortable because she'd be among women. There was one person she knew who'd faced the world and never let it change who she was, no matter what it threw at her.

Fabiana and Giuliana waited for a few minutes before Giuliana sensed the wolves outside coming to alert. She was out the door, calming the wolves to settle back down when Kalinda stepped out of her car. Her hair was in her signature bun, and she wore jeans that looked like they were poured on, with a t-shirt that had a pretty black woman on the front with an afro and multi-colored pick in her hair. *Black girl magic* was written underneath.

"Whose ass am I kicking?"

Giuliana laughed. "How are you feeling, Ales?"

Kalinda rolled her eyes. "I'm fine. I wasn't hurt, not that you can convince my mate of that." They headed inside the house as Kalinda continued. "I told him I'd press my heel into very sensitive places if he didn't let me out of the house."

Giuliana laughed and cut her eyes to Fabiana. Fabiana had tucked her paintings away and stood, wide-eyed, as she listened to Kalinda.

"He needs those places to keep you happy, Kalinda."

"So? He won't be able to enjoy me if he doesn't get out of my face."

"You talk to a male like that?"

Kalinda took in Fabiana. For a moment, something flashed in her gaze before she looked to Giuliana, who shook her head.

No, Fabiana wasn't who they thought she was.

Kalinda closed her eyes, lifting her hands toward Fabiana, and the woman shrunk back. "I'm sorry, I didn't mean to—"

"Don't run, Fabiana. You're stronger than that. And she won't hurt you. Remember what I said."

Fabiana stilled, but Giuliana could see her pulse jumping in her throat. Kalinda, it seemed, had finished her surface read of Fabiana and opened her eyes.

Zoey would have been better to coddle Fabiana, but that wasn't what she needed. She needed strength, acceptance, but she also had to learn how to deal with her fear. Kalinda had the ability, at least marginally, to use her empathic and manipulation gifts to read a person's emotions.

When Kalinda dropped her hands, she shook her head. "Gods, I want to break him."

Fabiana squeaked.

"That's the same reaction I had," Giuliana agreed.

Kalinda reached for Fabiana, leaving her hand hanging in the air when Fabiana didn't immediately shake it. "Let's start with my name. I'm Kalinda Thorton, mate to *Capo* Romano, head of the Trinity Council, and Ales."

Unsure, Fabiana took her hand. "I'm Fabiana Bianchi, unmated, and … I don't really know who I am."

"That's okay. Today, you're going to ride with the girls, and we're going to start to help you answer that."

Fabiana looked back and forth between Kalinda and Giuliana. "Are you serious?"

"As a heart attack. Silva has been itching to get out. Romano has extended his oppressive shit to her too. She'd like a change. Too bad Zoey is not up for a night out. But we'll see her when we get back."

"Zoey …" Fabiana let her voice trail off, shaking her head.

"Doesn't hold any grudges," Giuliana finished.

"That was for us to do, and we're standing here, aren't we?"

Take our hands, Fabiana. Don't break.

Giuliana willed the young woman, but she knew Fabiana would have to make her own decision. They couldn't force her one way or the other.

After what seemed like forever, Fabiana nodded. "Okay. I'd like that."

"First line of business: clothes. We're going to get you dressed," Giuliana said.

Fabiana looked down at herself. "I look fine."

"Clothes are armor, woman. Let's head to my place and go from there."

They pulled Fabiana from the house, and Giuliana whispered to the wolves at the door that Fabiana would be with her. She also sent a thought to her mate so he'd be aware.

Thank you, was all he sent back.

But his words were full of so much … so much emotion it took her breath away.

CHAPTER TWENTY

"You're an Alpha."

Pasquale knew this was coming the minute he'd shown his gifts when he'd helped Giuliana with Silva and Kalinda. He hadn't had a choice, and he wasn't about to change what he'd done. Through Giuliana, Kalinda's essence was held long enough for Zahara to reclaim Silva's soul and bring her back. He wouldn't regret helping with that.

But now, Dominic stood before him, his hands in his pockets with Romano at his side, glaring. He expected it. No Alpha male was supposed to hide who they were, and he'd broken that rule.

"Yes," Pasquale finally answered. For what it was worth, it was amazing to finally say it and finally have it out in the open.

Romano stepped forward. "How?"

And here was the part where shit would either go really bad … or horrible.

Or deadly. There is that.

Shut up, Snow.

"Primo Bianchi was my father."

Dominic's Alpha power blasted through the room, sending Romano to his knees. Pasquale reacted on instinct, wrapping his cooler, sharper Alpha power around the *Capo* and himself.

Romano blinked, coming to a stand. "How the hell …"

"I've been shielding for some time. It adds … control to my gift."

"I never knew Primo had a son."

Pasquale swung his attention back to Dominic. "He didn't want anyone to know. I had the chance to take his place, and he wasn't interested in sharing his power. If I stayed compliant and hid who I was, he wouldn't take it out on others."

Dominic frowned. "His pack?"

Pasquale was finally able to share what he never had before, not even with his mate. "It wasn't his first. I was … young and thought I could challenge him. I thought I could stop him from treating our people like his personal harem and stable to send out against others. I was so sure the ones who said they were on my side believed in me."

"They didn't," Romano surmised.

"Oh, only until their loved ones started dying. He destroyed the whole pack, except for me and his mate—Fabiana hadn't been born yet. And then he rebuilt. I learned to hide. And when Fabiana came … I couldn't let her face that."

"Fabiana could take anything. She was cut from your father's cloth."

Pasquale's warning growl filled the room. "She was beaten and controlled by my father for years. She was too afraid *not* to be just what he wanted—all so she could survive. She was a child made to play as a woman who was useful."

Dominic returned Pasquale's growl. "Be careful, pup."

"I won't let you disrespect her. I know what part she played in mating with you, but she was forced into it just like they tried to do with you, and she would have had even less choice than you."

Dominic nodded. "It wasn't exactly a normal mating. I can agree to that. But now, it's about what you want. Do you intend to take your pack?"

And that was the question, wasn't it? Pasquale been trying to come to the answer since his father's death, but he couldn't find one that didn't make him think he was stepping into shoes he didn't want to fill.

He shook his head. "I'm not ready to be Alpha."

Romano scoffed. "Sort of felt like it to me."

"I may be an Alpha male, but taking over a pack is a different story. I don't think I can do it. I can't be the Alpha my people need.

All they remember, all *we* remember, is my father. His cruelty, his abuse. Even now, we are on the outside of the Lombardi. We don't belong, and I don't know how to change it."

For a few minutes, the room was silent, the three men studying each other. Dominic looked to his *Capo*. "He could be Made."

Pasquale scoffed. "I'm already Made."

"Not in my pack, you aren't. As far as Lombardi, you are a scenter on retainer, but things can change."

"What do you mean?"

"You can be made a *Capo*."

Pasquale shot a look at Romano. "You already have a man for that."

"But he is not an Alpha. Taking the position, you'd be my second, and I would train you. When the time came, you'd take over your pack."

Pasquale shook his head. "I'm mated to Giuliana. I won't take her from her pack again. She is family here and looks to you as her brother. I don't want her separated from you."

"There is another option," Romano offered. "Let Pasquale become a *Capo* and have him run the Bianchi under your leadership, Alpha. He wouldn't have to take his pack away, but they'd be an extension. Really, they'd be Lombardi in every sense of the world, but they'd be his soldiers under you."

Dominic turned to Pasquale. "Could you do that? Give up a chance of a pack of your own to truly merge with mine and work under me?"

Snow?

I'm not against it. I've never wanted power like that, Alpha wolf or not. Red would be hurt.

She needs to stay home.

Agreed.

Will you be able to bow to another?

For Red and Giuliana, I would.

"Yes. I don't need a pack. It's not my claim. But … Romano?"

"Man, I'm mated to the leader of the Trinity Council. If this were a dick measuring contest, I'd win. You can become Dominic's second as *Capo*. I'd still be his *Capo* for his soldiers already within the pack. The position recognizes your Alpha status but keeps you within the fold."

Pasquale hadn't thought it was possible to find a way for his pack to be protected and be used together. He struggled to believe in the fragile hope blossoming in his heart.

"Is it," he cleared his throat. "Is it possible?"

"If you accept, yes. Your Alpha will only have to submit to mine. But I will not treat you like your father did. I am not here to brow-beat you into following me. It's your choice. We won't force you, and the wolves will adjust to your position."

Pasquale swallowed. His sister was with Giuliana, and he hadn't been able to do more than thank her. But now … this was more than he'd ever believed was possible.

Would you like to stay with your pack, if it can be done?

Her answer was instantaneous. *I'm going where you go, mate. We will figure it out.*

His decision was made. She would give it up for him, and the emotion filling his chest choked him. He never thought he'd find a mate *or* find a way to have his Alpha be accepted. Now, he'd found both.

Pasquale breathed deeply, pulling acceptance and change into his lungs. "Yes. I accept."

"Romano, get the cup and call the others who will bear witness."

Romano moved off, grabbing his phone, and Dominic stepped up to Pasquale. "I am not an easy man, and I will expect much from you. Giuliana is your mate, but she is *my* Enforcer. That will not change."

"You are asking me to stand aside if you have to punish her."

"I am not asking you," Dominic returned.

Pasquale gritted his teeth, knowing this was a test, a first mark for his Alpha to bow to another. Any wolf would struggle with his mate being hurt, and there was no way he'd be able to stop that urge to fight for her from coming out.

"I'm not going to sit to the side and let you break my mate, but I understand law."

"That's good enough. No man will ask another to ignore their instincts, but you have to be able to follow when necessary. I will give you this, if she is to be punished, you will be alerted to the extent. Agreed?"

"Yes, Alpha."

Dominic's eyes glittered. "Good. And you will only address me as such when we are in front of others. When we are alone, we are equals."

Pasquale swallowed, unable to say a word. He hadn't believed, hadn't hoped things would turn out the way they had. He'd been terrified he'd lose everything, that he'd be forced to take his pack into uncertain lands and be left astray. He'd believed he'd never have the mate of his heart standing beside him and would be cursed to know who she was but never claim her.

Things were not what he'd ever believed them to be.

His father had destroyed him in more ways than Pasquale had realized. Primo forced Pasquale to see shadows and the worst in everything.

Maybe …

Things may have not turned out the way they had if he'd come to Dominic in the first place, if he'd explained.

Pasquale looked at Dominic. "I won't hide anything from you again."

"Of that, I'm certain."

Doors opened, and wolves piled in dressed in suits, their guns gleaming at their sides. They stood tall, their heads canted to the side as they greeted Dominic. Each assumed a place surrounding Dominic and Pasquale, Romano coming to close the circle behind his Alpha.

"Today, we gain another brother. He stands before you in acceptance. Let him take the rite."

Dominic took the golden cup from Romano and held it in front of him. "Do you swear on death to uphold our laws? To not betray us? To not work against us?"

"I do."

"Do you pledge your allegiance to me and the Lombardi Pack?"

"I do."

Dominic let his fingers half-shift, thick claws springing from the tips. "Place you palm over the cup."

Pasquale did as Dominic asked. Swiftly, enough that it didn't hurt at first, Dominic sliced open his palm. Ruby-red blood welled into the gouge, spilling into the cup.

"Pasquale Bianchi will be a Lombardi wolf and *Capo*. He shall be second only to me, and he will rule the wolves of the former Bianchi.

They will no longer be called the Bianchi wolves. They will be Lombardi or Pasquale's wolves. They will no longer be on the outside but will be important to our defenses. He has taken the rite of *Omérta* and will die if he changes. He will be inked with our blood and our mark."

Pasquale's healing kicked in, sealing the cut, and the other wolves also cut their palms and stepped forward to bleed into the cup. Once finished, they passed the cup around, each taking a small sip before one wolf produced a tattoo gun.

"Bare your arm, Pasquale."

As requested, Pasquale removed his jacket and unbuttoned his shirt so he could pull out his arm. He stood silently as the gun traced over his skin. A crescent moon with a howling wolf, made in the blood of the head males of the Lombardi, came to life on his skin.

With a nod, the tattoo artist stepped back and went to another little tray of color, this one a brilliant blue.

"He is also an Alpha and will be recognized as such. No man but me may direct him."

"Yes, Alpha," the men responded.

The tattoo artist came back and gave Pasquale's wolf blue eyes.

"The blue is for your people. For your power. As you are an Alpha, Giuliana is now an Alpha mate. She will be afforded the same respect as one should. The only woman of this pack to outrank her shall be Zoey. Is that understood?"

"Yes, Alpha," they answered.

The tattoo was finished, already healed because of his ability, and Pasquale stood proud. He was accepted. He was Alpha. He was part of a pack.

"One last step, so that we may call you brother," Dominic warned.

Pasquale knew this one, remembered the pleasure Primo got from ripping him apart and breaking him. Pasquale sank to his feet, a blank mask on his face even as his insides went crazy.

I will protect you, Pasquale. Give over to me.

I have to face it.

Your mind can't yet. Your Alpha will understand.

Let me try.

Dominic stepped behind Pasquale and raked his claws across Pasquale's back. The fire burned, pressing deep. Skin split, the fire spreading through Pasquale's insides.

But then Dominic was finished, and another brother was there.

Pasquale opened shocked eyes. They weren't ripping to the bone. They weren't trying to abuse him. While the swipes hurt, they didn't cripple him.

He looked up, and his gaze clashed with Dominic's.

"I am not your father," Dominic whispered.

Pasquale stayed like that, his gaze locked on his Alpha as every wolf in the room added their mark to his skin. At their depth, nothing would scar. It was an honorary act to show he wouldn't fight his people; he wouldn't retaliate out of anger and rage. He'd accept, this one time, being on his knees before them.

We have a good home, Snow added.

Yes.

When it was over, Dominic gripped his shoulders and helped him stand. "Welcome, brother. Though, you may want to get changed and burn the shirt. Your mate will come after my head if she thinks I've hurt you."

Pasquale chuckled. "She has a way of ignoring Alphas."

"Don't I know it. That probably should have been a clue as to who you were."

"I still win."

Dominic and Pasquale frowned over at Romano.

"The dick measuring contest. I still win."

Pasquale rolled his eyes. "Apparently, your balls sweep the floor."

"Of course. I can barely walk with these fucking things. Sometimes, I have Dominic—"

"Shut up, Romano."

The admonishment may have been quick and harsh from Dominic, but it was filled with warmth. Family. They were a family. If nothing else, Pasquale could be more than thankful for that.

I love you, mate. Thank you for bringing me home.

I-I love you too. Giuliana's voice was hesitant, filled with awe, and he could nearly see her face damp with tears.

I love you too!

Red. Pasquale smiled at the wolf in his head. *Of course, Red. You're the most beautiful wolf in the world.*

You see? He thinks I'm pretty. We have a good male. Can we mate now?

Be home when I get there, sweet cheeks.

Snow ... did you just call me ... sweet cheeks?
Payback for the "dude".
I'm going to shave you.
Just be home, mate, as you were told. You're welcome to try it then.

Pasquale snorted. *Snow, I think Giuliana and I should be able to make that choice.*

You want to mate, so does she. Simple.

Giuliana's warm chuckle fill his head. *I'll race you, big boy.*

Big boy. I see us tossing names back and forth from now on.

You got it, liver lumps.

Oh, I'm going to get you for that one.

You're on.

Nodding to Dominic, Pasquale streaked out of the room and out the front door in record time. To his mate. To the rest of his life.

Epilogue

He'd been wrong. So fucking wrong.

The reality of that—what he'd lost and would never get back—nearly paralyzed him. When does one ever think their memories can't be trusted? Was anything he'd ever remembered true?

Heath—because calling himself Kieran made him sick to his stomach—clutched a spell phone in his bloody hand, coughing up more of the red fluid until it dribbled down his chin. He couldn't have been completely wrong, could he?

Kieran had taken Kalinda hostage. *Kieran* had told his best friend he'd see him on the other end of his gun. And *Kieran* had royally destroyed everything Heath had ever believed he could have. Heath thought he'd left all that behind.

The anger.
The resentment.
The loneliness.
After finding Cin …

Heath closed his eyes, picturing the slender woman with her quirky style, sharp tongue, and beautiful jewelry. He'd thought *maybe* he could find peace. But then she was taken too. Lorenzo had come along, and she'd found conventional love. A love where the other person didn't have to hide or lie about who they were.

Cin may have never known who he was, but she'd been able to sense he hadn't been completely truthful with her. With bloody fingertips, he clicked to his photo gallery on his phone, determined to find something real. He still had everything—the texts, pictures, and call log. Everything to prove Lorenzo and Cin had been real. That Heath hadn't been alone in the world after losing so much in the Fae lands.

But had he truly lost everything?

Silva's complete surprise and soul-deep cry of innocence had stayed Heath's hand so he hadn't administered the killing blow. But it was probably too late anyway. He'd fucked up so much. Cin would never forgive him. Lorenzo would never trust him again.

He'd lost … everything.

He forced his fingers to work, to dial the one number he could always remember by heart. It was futile, of course, but he had to try. Anything. Something to make it right. The phone rang loud in his ear, a bang against his eardrums.

Punishment for having done so much to fuck those who'd stood behind him.

"Heath?"

Lorenzo's voice was disbelieving, a prayer, a hope.

When the pack returned home, he had no doubt they'd tell him what had happened. But for a short span of time, he'd still be Heath's friend.

"Hey, man."

Lorenzo must have dropped the phone. It rattled on the other end before Lorenzo was back. "Where the fuck are you? I thought … *we* thought you were dead."

There was hurt and agony in that one stressed word. *We.* Cin and Lorenzo.

"I … Fuck. I don't know how to do this."

"Just tell me where you are. I'll come get you. We'll figure it out."

Yeah. Because that was Lorenzo—forgiving, caring, the best friend in the world. But Heath had betrayed him.

"Listen. When Romano comes home, you're going to find out things about me I never wished you would."

"Heath—"

"I'm sorry. For all of it. I just … I was so messed up. I wanted revenge. I wanted … to destroy who I thought had destroyed what I'd been."

Heath coughed, the action wrecking his chest, and he wheezed. Dying was painful, and he didn't give a shit what anyone said otherwise. It soaked up every thought in his head, pushed him to get the words out before he couldn't. He may not survive this call, but at least … at least he'd give Lorenzo some peace.

"I'm going to fix it. I don't know how, and it may take the rest of my life, but I will. Don't tell Cin I'm still alive. Let her believe I'm gone. Let me be dead for her. Just … promise me you'll be everything she ever needed. Everything she wished I could be but couldn't."

Lorenzo was silent on the other end of the line, and Heath didn't know what else to say. He may not have loved Cin the way she wanted him to, the way she'd hoped he would eventually—before she met Lorenzo. But he did care. He did want someone to take care of her.

He'd never loved her because he had nothing in his heart but pain.

But that wasn't her fault, and he didn't want her to suffer.

"How bad is it, Heath?"

"Enough to put a bullet in my head."

"Whatever it takes, no matter how long, you fix it. Do you understand me? Fix it."

"I will."

The line went dead, and that was probably for the best anyway. He was so fucking tired.

Just take me home. Let me die having seen home one last time.

It was a pathetic prayer. One told to him when he was young. At death, for the Unseelie, they got one wish. One act of kindness for a life of pain they were forced to endure because of the sins of their forefathers.

One wish to pray for and be granted.

Most, he figured, probably begged for their life. But Heath didn't want his life without knowing what really happened all those years ago. Why he'd suffered, or if he even had. But he wasn't so naïve to believe he'd be given that chance, so he prayed to see home. To feel that magic surround him as he faded to the great beyond.

Instead, the Chaos Realm opened, the portal whipping and reaching for him as he lolled to the side. He shot his middle finger at it.

Even that was a lie. Fucking figures.

You wanted truth, Kieran of the Shadow. Come find your truth.

He forced his head up off the ground. "Who *are* you?"

No one. Everyone. Do you want your truth, or not?

His heart slugged on, each passing second a struggle just to keep working. "Yes, I do."

Help her get what you seek.

"Her?"

Black tendrils sprung from the darkness, gripping his arms and ankles. He bellowed, fire streaking through his gut and clutching his heart in an iron fist.

Help her.

The words mixed with his screams as he was dragged into the Chaos Realm and the world faded to nothing but agony.

DO YOU WANT MORE OF THE PORTAL CITY PROTECTORS?

Mated to the Capo:
Curvy earth witch meets dangerously sexy wolf.
Will Zoey accept Dominic's claim before it's too late?
https://books2read.com/MatedCapo

Mated to the Enforcer:
It seems like everyone in Encantado is out to get Kalinda.
Can Romano claim her in time?
https://books2read.com/MatedEnforcer

Mated to the Prince:
Pasquale is super sexy … and Giuliana can't stand the sight of him.
Or can she?
https://books2read.com/MatedPrince

Fated to the Traitor:
Things are heating up in Encantado, and Heath is right in the middle of it … along with a mysterious Fae princess.
https://books2read.com/FatedTraitor

Mated to the Chaos:
Carlo has been lost for so long, but the past might hold the key to his future.
https://books2read.com/MatedChaos

Mated to the Moon:
Fabiana has struggled to figure out where she belongs, but Adonis is determined to help her find her place.
https://books2read.com/MatedMoon

ABOUT THE AUTHORS

Georgette

Georgette St. Clair writes hot, sexy romances starring Alpha heroes. The road to love may be rocky and fraught with peril (and humor and scorchtastic sex and healthy heapings of snark), but her shifters will stop at nothing to claim the women they love.

Georgette has worn many hats in life: newspaper reporter, EMT, internet marketer, cocktail waitress, temp, nurse's aide (not in chronological order).

When she's not rescuing fur-babies, she spends her days in a fantasy universe where she nudges her smart-mouthed, take-no-gruff heroines onto paths which will set them on a collision course with true love.

FOLLOW GEORGETTE:

Facebook
www.facebook.com/georgettewrites
Newsletter
georgettewrites.com/newsletter
Goodreads
smarturl.it/GR-Ginger
Website
georgettewrites.com

LeTeisha

Writing professionally since 2008, LeTeisha Newton's love of romance novels began long before it should have. After spending years sneaking reads from her grandmother's stash, she finally decided to pen her own tales. As many will do during their youth, she bounced from fantasy, urban literature, mainstream, interracial, paranormal, heterosexual, and LGBT works until she finally rested in contemporary romance.

LeTeisha is all about deep angst and angry heroes who take a bit more loving to smooth their rough edges. Love comes in many sizes, shapes, and colors, as well as with—or without—absolute beauty and fairy tale sweetness. She writes the darker tales because life is hard … but love is harder.

FOLLOW LETEISHA:

Facebook
smarturl.It/fb-leteisha

Website
smarturl.It/leteisha-website

Goodreads
smarturl.It/gr-leteisha

Newsletter
smarturl.It/lt-newsletter

Printed in Great Britain
by Amazon